AF484952

Acclaim for *The Night Hides with a Knife*

"A respectable collection of short stories written in elegant and piquant style and demonstrates profound insight into human psychology."

— *Jury, Association of Nigerian Authors*
/Spectrum Prize for Fiction

"With this first collection of short stories, Nduka Otiono takes us on an impressive, multi-textual journey of resourcefulness and creativity that combines the best of the oral and scribal in Nigeria's literary culture: traditional storytelling strategies and conventional narrative forms are overlaced with a fragmentary, postmodern reflexivity; the voice propels the pen, only to get trapped in the tape recorder."

— *Harry Garuba, poet and Professor,*
University of Cape Town, South Africa

"...a synthesis of the archetypal forms of the oral tradition with modern urban realism."

— *D.S. Izevbaye, Emeritus Professor of*
English and Fellow of the Nigerian Academy of Letters

"Several years of craftsmanship have transformed the ten short stories in this collection into gems of chiseled prose... In these stories, we see the dreams of an entire generation reaching up for the lights or sinking into the fetid swamp of the nation's grave."

— *The Guardian*

"...challenges the stereotype notion that modern African prose lacks experimental forms. The...collection defies, and indeed straddles genre classification."
— *Monitor Review*

"There is...a deeply autobiographical tenor in the short stories, for they tend to proclaim the geography of Otiono's times... The greatest achievement...is his deep and significant power of observation, in the surprising detail of his narrative."
— *Vanguard*

"*The Night Hides with a Knife* is a collection of familiar and somewhat absurd experiences...Nduka Otiono is unique because his exploration of experiences is stylized. In essence, he is a stylist at heart: manner matters a lot to him."
— *TheNews Magazine*

"Otiono's painstaking assemblage of the loom of existence with its strands drawn from the nation's socio-political realities is the staple of everyday life... By giving free reign to his imagination and inventiveness and by drawing on the rich and time-tested resources of the oral tradition and heritage of African literature, Otiono makes *The Night Hides with a Knife* an irresistible work in the narrative genre."
— *Weekend Times*

"Otiono's ability to capture true life experiences manifests in stories like 'A Will to Survive', 'Wings of Rebellion'. . ."
— *Sunday Times*

"The issue in Nigerian fiction is no longer that of good and evil. Our experience in the postmodern and post-colonial times has driven us beyond those fringes. As *The Night Hides with a Knife* has clearly symbolized, the issue is that of the beautiful and the ugly, the dark and the light, a distinction which must remain foregrounded in the consciousness of every Nigerian in order to remind us of our vanishing beauty and dream as a people.
— *Frank Uche Mowah, writer and former Head of Department of English, Ambrose Alli University, Nigeria*

"These stories are experimental, displaying an awareness of modern currents and a delicate narrative sensitivity to autochthonous structures… Part of the assets [the author] displays are his sharp, smooth-flowing prose and his sense of adventure and experimentation…He is at his best when exploiting the structures of oral performance."
— *Wumi Raji, author of* Long Dreams in Short Chapters: Essays in African Postcolonial Literary, Cultural and Political Criticisms.

The Night Hides With a Knife

Short Stories

Nduka Otiono

New Horn Press
&
Mace Associates Limited

First published in Nigeria by:

New Horn Press Ltd
in association with
Critical Forum
Ibadan.

First published 1995

ISBN: 978-325-18-3-X

Revised edition 2021
Published by New Horn Press Ltd.
in conjunction with
Mace Associates Limited
1 Sanyaolu Street
Oregun, Lagos, Nigeria.

ISBN: 978-978-8033-59-2

www.ndukaotiono.com

This book is a work of fiction. All characters portrayed in this book
are the author's fictional creation. Any resemblance to actual persons,
living or dead, or actual events, is purely coincidental.

To
Bene and Mike -
the twin seeds from
whom I sprouted

In Memoriam:
Nweke Momah -
Singer of tales,
oral historian and comedian
who rejoined the earth
but left the art
behind

&

Sesan Ajayi
and other victims
of night that hides
with a knife.

Contents

Foreword

Iᴛ used to be argued that creative writing thrives only under certain favourable social or economic conditions. But now it seems that art will find a way of expressing itself even in the age of SAP, for each generation must speak with its own voice and not suck the art of its predecessors endlessly. In Nigeria at the present time, writing goes on without ceasing, especially among undergraduates, journalists and teachers who express themselves in a variety of literary forms. Nduka Otiono, whose writing career began at Ibadan where he was an undergraduate between 1984 and 1987 when I first knew him, has been interested in the storytelling form.

Storytelling is probably the most accessible and most popular of African traditional as well as modern literary forms. In its most basic form, the traditional oral tale is driven by an idealistic vision and a strong moral impulse which enables the teller to refine and assimilate different historical and social experiences into a pattern of enduring and repeatable incidents. Writing can and does often reduce the tale to its bare pattern; the vigour of the traditional tale tends to be lost in print, for it is the oral medium that stimulates the dramatic energy of traditional storytelling.

Although traditional storytelling will always survive in forms like the anecdote and the yarn, the true storytelling form of our own age is the non-oral short story. This new form reflects a dual cultural inheritance, the African and the European, and these are often present as elements of the fantastic and the realistic, respectively. The realistic short story is largely the product of a new kind of society with its urban base and its European imports: the printing press is the main instrument of its communication; its offices and factories are the key to its economic life and its employment opportunities; the bar and the brothel are the places of entertainment and escape from the psychological pressures of city life.

Otiono is aware of these dynamics of social change. In this collection of stories written in the seven-year period between 1986 and 1992, the focus shifts between two fictional modes. There is, on the one hand, the recognisable urban realism of the stories which open and close the collection. Other stories of this type (for example, "Escapade" and "Fatal Birth") go even farther: the narrator is fascinated by the seamy and melodramatic experiences which contemporary city life has forced on its victims. This type of story thrives on the witty exchange, the clever pun, and the frequent code-switching that are common features of the speech of Nigerian city streets.

But there is another kind of story—one which attempts a synthesis of the archetypal forms of the oral tradition with modern urban realism. In a story like "Wings of Rebellion," Otiono seeks an insight into the problem, "what happens to narrative as it travels from the oral to the written form?" The statement summarises a basic concern of Otiono's writing. But the political awareness reflected in the allusions to national and international events takes the stories beyond this formal interest. And the awareness is not that of political matters only. There is also a feeling for the physical environment whose sights, smells and sounds create the atmosphere in the stories. But the awareness of contemporary society in the stories is strongest in the author's sense of community with other writers, many of them his friends and contemporaries. Their works partly provide the allusions for his stories. As a result of Otiono's belief that "experimentation is the fresh breath of art," elements of oral art, contemporary affairs and personal relationships are incorporated into his writing, experimentally.

September 1995
D.S. Izevbaye
Department of English,
University of Ibadan,
Ibadan, Nigeria

Acknowledgements

I am profoundly grateful to:

- Professor Chikwenye Okonjo-Ogunyemi, for providing the bridge that led me to Ibadan in 1984.
- The English Department, University of Ibadan, for very rewarding creative writing workshops and intellectual nourishment.
- Professor Isidore Okpewho, for being an excellent mentor and inspirer.
- Professor D.S. Izevbaye, for writing the Foreword.
- My siblings: Phil, Val, Fabian and Mike (Jr), for appreciating the artistic loop of the blood knot.
- *ANA Review, Nigerian Tribune, Idoto* and *Echoes,* journal of the Storytellers' Club, University of Ibadan, for first publishing four of the stories in this collection.
- The *Nigerian Observer* reporter (I cannot recall his name now) whose article on prostitution provided me with the "Vicky angle"

for anchoring "The Will to Survive."
– The writers and artists from whose works I
have borrowed epigraphs and other touch-
stones incorporated into this book.
– The *Obu Isi Bia Ani Ikwa* Group of Og-
washi-Uku, and Nweke Momah's *Otu Onye
Loshe Onwu Oje Nwayo* Group of Ubu-
lu-Uku, Delta State, for their enlightening
oral performances that I recorded during
my fieldwork in the 1980s.
– Professor Abiola Irele and Professor Dipo
Irele, for originally publishing this book on
their imprints, New Horn Press & Critical
Forum.

Author's note for the new edition

THE paradox of Time is such that half a century sounds like such a long time yet being absorbed in the everyday business of life can make it begone with the wind. When this collection, *The Night Hides with a Knife*, was first published in 1995, the present time loomed ahead like eternity and belonged to a different century. Indeed, 2021 sounded like a sci-fi age to a sprouting writer straining for sunlight to grow.

The Night went out of print shortly after its initial print run of one thousand copies. The speed with which the original edition disappeared upon publication apparently caught both the young author and the small indie press which published it unprepared. The intervening years seem to have flown meteorically, leaving the author trapped in that portrait of the artist as a scholar which Isidore Okpewho theorizes in his inaugural lecture titled *A Portrait of the Artist as a Scholar* (1990). So that the years spent pursuing scholarship and a second career as an academic, after working for fifteen years as a journalist in Nigeria, prolonged the author's distraction from the fate of *The Night* and his fiction writing muse. As Okpewho frames it, when the artist is engaged in scholarly pursuits, his creative faculties appear to go on holiday, and vice versa.

The silver jubilee anniversary of *The Night* has happily awakened the long overdue need to repossess the book and its cast of spectral characters and their sometimes-baffling experiences and actions. Re-reading these stories now leaves me feeling like a stranger to their youthful creator. The temptation was strong to re-write large chunks of each story to "update" them, as it were. But I resisted the temptation, preferring to offer the reader the original world of the narrators between the late 1980s and early 1990s.

But besides the retention of the original universe of the stories, this 25th anniversary edition comes with a new cover, a new Afterword by Frank Uche Mowah of blessed memory, and selected excerpts from the critical reviews at the time of its publication. I have also undertaken some editorial changes, essentially to fix awkward errors in the rendering of the first life of the book.

Much of the editorial work for the renewal of the book was done by Fifi Edem, my publishing and editorial consultant. I am grateful to her for her patience and professionalism. I thank Ifesinachi Johnpaul Nwadike, my research assistant, and his crew—Jennifer Chisom Azubuike and Dhee Sylvester—for the beautiful cover design. I acknowledge the editorial support of Emma Bider, whose familiarity with my style through different projects is an asset that has served me well, especially in the final stages of publishing this edition. I would also like to thank Richard Mammah, journalist, publisher and proprietor of Mace Associates Limited, for his commitment to co-publishing this edition.

A Will To Survive

The decadence in the air
grates on the iron petal
my will to survival.

– Odia Ofeimun

S URVIVAL is a cruel battle of wits. At least so it was on the second day of January last year. That day, the cold harmattan wind was a blunt knife cutting benumbed bodies busy hustling for tickets or some other articles at a mass transit terminus in the city. One of the bodies was that of a decrepit and ghostly man. He was begging for alms. Behind the pair of his weird-looking glasses, the man's sunken eyes stared blankly and coldly at the world. They gave him the gaunt appearance of an aged scholar. Even more so when the contours which marked his face with seeming lines of wisdom were considered. On his head sat a weather-beaten black hat which colour-rioted with the brown shirt and rumpled pair of green trousers he wore. On his feet was a pair of tattered rubber slippers of different colours—white on the left foot and red on the right foot. His left hand held an improvised walking stick and a black polythene bag containing multifarious items. The petit, forty-something-year-old man meandered through the crowd, groping his way with the improvised walking stick. It was as if he was hoping that the manifest signs of despair on his face and in his movements would register with at least someone.

Nobody seems to notice me, he thought, chewing his lips bitterly. *Or could it be that they've all spent so much money during the season's festivities that they do not have any left to spare a helpless, old man like me? Or could it be a mark of the bad times which through retrenchment claimed my humble job as a cleaner in Township Secondary School's library about eighteen months ago? Well, whatever it may be, somebody has to pay for this I-don't-care attitude and the neglect of an old man by these prospective travellers.*

Still groping his way, Old Man wormed into the crowd of passengers around the counter from where tickets were bought. Nobody seemed to notice him still. Not exactly that, though. For someone did mistake him for one of the throng of travellers struggling to obtain the limited number of tickets on sale. It was a tall, unemployed young man approaching his mid-thirties. He wore an aging black coat over a wine-coloured check shirt and a pair of red velvet trousers. The slit of the pocket was ajar; one could see some of its contents. In the right pocket of the coat was haphazardly stuffed a small tin of Robb, some sheets of tissue paper, and two hundred and fifty naira.

The mischievous ambler inched his way closer to the unemployed graduate who was engrossed in obtaining a ticket for his trip to the Federal Capital Territory. In the tension of that moment, the crafty man, peering into the now half-open pocket of the young man's coat, slipped his right hand into it and skilfully stole the two hundred and fifty naira and sneaked away from the scene.

Just then it struck the young man to feel his pocket. But he could not locate the two crispy notes. He looked into the pocket and was stunned to find it emptied of the money he had tucked into it. It struck him that that haggard beggar who had just flitted through the crowd could be the culprit. Incensed with anger, he accosted the man.

"Ehm, what did you go to do there just now . . . I mean, where tickets are being sold?"

"Oh, I never reach there. How a blind, helpless old man like me fit move for dat kind crowd wey go dey for dat kind spot?"

"Okay, may I search you?"

"Ah, oya now!"

The young man surveyed Old Man suspiciously, taking in details of places where he could possibly have hidden his lost money. He peeped into the black polythene bag and saw, among other things, a fifty kobo note. He was confused. He could not fathom where the man could so quickly have tucked away his only sum of money. The man's total surrender to a search bewildered him even further. He mused with tears welling up in his eyes, *won't it be preposterous to molest such a decrepit, innocuous man? Well, even if he has my money, doesn't he, a living-dead man, need it more than I do? But to opt for obtaining it is by all means . . . But, again, he might not even be the culprit. Who knows? O Lord, forgive me!*

As the young man turned his back, the crafty beggar felt the cuff of the left sleeve of his worn-out shirt. Satisfied that the money was safely there, he congratulated himself. As he resumed the search for yet another victim, he justified his callous business by recalling a fragment of what Vicky, a resident of his favourite brothel at Ugbague Street, had once said to him: "But if you have to survive, somehow you have to do anything to save yourself from going to pieces."

The Night Hides With A Knife
(for Fabian)

behind the clenched, white
barns all afternoon the night
hides with a knife.

– Derek Walcott

I T was the night penultimate to the close of
a year. On the horizon a sad, solemn star
was blinking in a bleak sky. Leaning on a
decaying tree in the backyard of a dilapidated mud
house beside the road was a form more solemn than
the fading star, a young boy in a trance-like state.
The gloom that wrapped his face united with the
darkness and the bleak sky. He stood still, imagin-
ing a shrub of *mimosa pudica* opening like a clenched
fist. He was still and hollow like the haunting space
above him; hollow like the middle of a pawpaw. He
kept still, as if afraid. He appeared to be brooding
over a nerve-racking problem. He stood still like
the dying tree he was leaning on, its branches dried,

its roots rotting. He seemed to be listening to the monotone of his heartbeat.

Footfalls of approaching forms roused him. He dipped one of his dehydrated hands into the left pocket of his dirty acid-wash jeans and fondled the last jumbo wrap of cannabis therein. He thought bitterly of his life as being a heap of disappointments, a series of minor explosions whose dying echoes were settling at. . .

"Ejiofor, stop there!" a voice hollered.

At that moment, thunder peals, rumblings, lightning flashes wracked Ejiofor's thoughts with the urgency of foam out of the mouth of an epileptic in a fit. Even then, Ejiofor Onwuka's friends continued to chat about the party they were strolling home from. Somehow, he was not part of the discussions. Instead, he was buried in thoughts of the mystery called 'night' . . . that emblem of the shared condition of all humankind; that metaphor of the unknown; that portion of unclear reasoning; that hazy moment before death; that . . . and the ideas continued to roll in his mind with the leisure of a smoker puffing out his first stream of inhaled smoke.

"Hey! Ol'boy! Ejiofor Onwuka! You cut my

necklace, come steal my two hundred *card** the other day. Vomit am now or. . ."

"I don't know you," Ejiofor protested in a rather muffled voice, peering as much as he could into the gaunt face of the boy from the shadows. The refracted rays of a low voltage electric bulb could not illumine the boy properly. However, Ejiofor was able to catch a glimpse of the boy's eyes which shone menacingly.

"You no know who?" thundered the scraggy boy, his *area boy** guttural rasp reverberating in the still night whose repose was hacked by the exchange between him and Ejiofor.

"But what's all this?" Ejiofor pressed further, still assessing the frail-looking boy. The boy's dark complexion, his pendulous ear and the scar on his right cheek registered instantly in Ejiofor's memory.

Meanwhile, a small party of spectators had begun to gather at the scene to watch the New Year Eve's real-life movie. And the lean boy whose mind was laden with untold fury, swung a trained fist in the direction of Ejiofor's head. Instinctively, Ejiofor blocked it with his right arm. The boy charged at him, throwing in blows like a blindfolded vagrant, cursing and tearing the shirt of the calm Ejiofor. But how calm would a man attacked by a near-lunatic at the edge of a water well remain?

"Leave them! Leave them!" Some enthusiastic spectators rent the air with cacophonous voices, urging a 'free fight' in the impromptu ring they had formed.

"No, it's dangerous. Can't you see the water well behind them?" somebody protested, attempting to dispossess the charging boy of a chunk of wood he had picked up. In a frenzy, the dusty boy unleashed a semi-circular swing with the piece of wood in the direction of Ejiofor's head. Ejiofor, like an intelligent martial arts exponent, thrust his left arm in the direction of the missile, side-stepping simultaneously. It hit him on his ulna with a cracking sound.

"Lord!" He winced, biting his lips and shutting his eyes for a fraction of the fragile moment. He was standing right at the edge of the well with its top barely covered by a few sticks; he was standing there like Christ on the precipice on which Satan tempted him. He stood there in that fragile moment, his courage enkindled by the fire of survival. He dived at the boy who was bending down to pick up his fallen weapon. Ejiofor charged at him with the fury of a wounded hyena, his mind now bereft of any sense of danger. He beat up the boy randomly, slapping, hitting, kicking, and spurting out venom: "You stink . . . you mad murderer . . ." The boy tottered like a feather being piloted by wind. "You're rotten and I'll clean you up—of the liquor and the *ganja*.* I'll send you either to the orthopaedic hospital or to the cemetery. . ."

"It's okay, Ofor," one of his friends pleaded.

"Leave him to his fate. Let's go," another added.

But the boy did not budge. As if injected with a new dose of strength and confidence, he charged again towards Ejiofor, beads of blood trickling out of his nostrils.

"Run! Run! R-u-u-u-n! It's no use fighting somebody who's lost all value for his life," someone sounded a panicky warning.

And Ejiofor obeyed. As he sped off, the possessed boy charged toward Ejiofor's friend, the one who had advised him to run. Helped by a colleague of his who had arrived on the scene, the boy pummelled his new victim. Beside the open water well, they 'donated' blows freely to him, almost tipping him into the well.

As if content with the measure they had doled out to the victim, the possessed boys chased after

Ejiofor and his other friend. But they were not swift-footed enough.

Just then a cock crowed. Wisps of dust raised at the scene of the fight began to settle. A chill breeze hurried past like some unpleasant sound. Only a blot of the twinkling star could be sighted in the distant sky. A massive, ominous group of clouds was tucking in the night's last fire. Against this background, the shady boy began to retreat with the vexed mien of a warlord who had been disgraced in a battle.

Meanwhile, two of Ejiofor's friends, the one who had been thoroughly brutalised included, were marching to safety through the tarred road in front of the mud house behind which a fighting arena had been created a fractured moment ago. The boy ran towards them.

"You, why you abuse my a'ntie?"

Rushing, he swung his arm twice, stabbing one of the surprised youths twice in the back. As if satisfied with that, he rushed after the other one who was yet to pull himself together, stabbing away at him.

"If you no run I go *mud** you o," the attacker threatened to kill in his characteristic Warri township argot. His eyes were blazing like metal in a blacksmith's furnace. "After that, you go tell your God how fight dey be and. . ."

But the appearance of two policemen reaching out for him shocked the words off his mouth. And the thought of spending the New Year's Eve and Day—and God knew how many more days—in police cell flitted through his mind like an accident.

Crossfire

Alone in his torment man
does an ellipsoidal dance
like a demon borne on the
branch of the god-tree.

– Syl Cheney-Coker

A*ND there was a stormy riot in the sky as he transcended the world. Seeing a generous man throw a bone to a starving dog. The bone was white. Except for little blotches of meat . . .*

PEALS of thunder loud enough to deafen a man roused him from a disturbing dream. As he lay supine on the rickety six-spring bed, he coughed and swallowed the phlegm. Then he tried to sort out his beleaguered life, but his reasoning coursed uncontrollably through a delta of unpleasant thoughts, which emptied into an overwhelming sea of disillusion. Still, he kept struggling with himself to maintain a train of thought.

"I ought to be a man!" he said aloud. "I should think properly," he concluded in a voice rasped by grief.

Flashes of light startled him. He rose with some effort from the creaking bed and suddenly slumped onto the bare, dirty, and cold floor. He yawned. He stared at the dark and blank room as if in a torpor. Around him, mosquitoes saturated with his own blood loitered and crooned a dirge. He had clapped his hands and slapped himself to depopulate them until his body began to ache. And, in his utter helplessness, he surrendered. The flashes of lightning forcing their way into his room through the gaping slits in the half-ceiled roof were sufficient to reveal the wet patches of blood on his palms.

He touched a patch on his left palm with his right index finger. It was slightly thick and slimy, like pus oozing out of an old boil. He rubbed his palms together, then tried to shut his eyes against the ulcerous sight which confronted him. He drifted into sleep with the upper region of his back arched against the bed, his hands spread out like the Saviour's hands as He hung on the Cross. It would have been one of those kinds of sleep in which the individual finds himself in the twilight zone between waking and sleeping, such a sleep that serves as delightful food to nourish the individual's soul—like a scherzo. But his was one in which his subconscious zoomed through a maze of dizzying experiences, like the tortured eyes of a destitute through a bag of rags...

Something was eating EKE's intestines and sucking up his pale blood, and he was unresisting.

"But why are you doing this to me?" the words slipped out of his subconscious.

"Why am I doing this to you or why are *we* doing this to you?" retorted one of the monstrous creatures with a sardonic smile.

"Yes, why? What have I done to you all?"

"You're betraying your ignorance. How often does one give cause to the misfortunes that befall one in life?"

The rhetorical response caught him unprepared. It incised very deep marks inside him. He yawned and shuddered. And the faceless creatures continued to explore his bowels and veins anatomically. When they had eaten up his intestines and sucked up his blood, they sought to sever his head. But somehow, the glow of the long and curved heated knife startled him out of the dreadful dream.

Flat, empty, and drained like a squashed mosquito, he waved his left hand weakly and meaninglessly over his chest. Then he froze like a corpse—he was a mere living corpse waiting to be lowered six feet into the earth, he thought. He felt his pulse as if unsure it still beat. His heart was ticking, ticking like a cell-powered chronometer about to stop because its cellular life was almost spent.

He fought hard to unravel the meaning of the 'morning mare.' But he was all the more lost in the depths of that very effort.

"Is such a strange, incomprehensible and forbidden experience possible?" he asked himself as his heartbeat slowed down like an ebbing wave. He felt like a setting sun, and then became curiously happy.

"After all," he soliloquised, "my life has been torn piecemeal by the forces of evil, the forces of death." He felt completely alone in a world peopled by all sorts of strange things. "I loathe my life," he concluded grimly.

As he sat absent-mindedly on the cold and unsympathetic floor trying to steer his thoughts, he instinctively rubbed his eyes, as if to prevent yet another slip into a bizarre trance. He yawned again, muttering some unintelligible words. A bang on the door—if it could be called a door—jolted him into harsh reality. He noticed that the rays of the sun peering into the tiny room as if they were mocking his inner solitude were becoming intense. As he rose from the floor and strolled towards the door, a weak current of air stroked the bruises around his neck. It soothed him like Freedom balm. As he walked lazily to the door, Egunje, the warder—so fondly called because of his penchant for taking bribes— was manipulating the lock of the welded iron bars that made up the door.

STEPHEN Uwaoma was, in his early twenties, a remarkably intelligent young man who could have achieved quite a lot in life. He was dark and lean and had a fat, egg-shaped head which was disproportionate to his rather brief and frail frame. He carried his fat head like a burden. His egg head was decorated with a pair of anxious hazel eyes below a shrub of eyebrows. Also adorning his oval face was a slightly flat nose and an unhappy strip of taut lips which appeared forever unready for a smile. A strip of moustache resembling Herbert Macaulay's clung stubbornly to the flesh just above his upper lip. Bristles clustered around his chin and his ambitious Adam's apple. Stephen's mien impressed one like a sage's.

Along the narrow veranda, he, together with other prisoners, walked hungrily behind the warder. Their dirty white uniforms were more like rags that seemed to have been rent by the hollering thunder and charged lightning. Within Stephen, who seemed not to notice the others, the unfortunate events which had dominated his life were raging, seeking expression as the sky was then doing, unbuttoning its grief to humanity. But Stephen's remained sealed up in his mind. He felt totally alone: without even a companion before whom to open the cage of his tired life. And he wanted to free that bird of wild thoughts entrapped therein, chirping endsongs resembling the cacophony of a henhouse. And his heart continued to pound like the staccato bursts of a machine gun. And it was as if his sanity was deserting him because he had not given the tortured bird a way to escape.

He began to hear voices hollering at random in his head; or was it in his mind? He heard a Sophist philosopher he had read somewhere shouting repeatedly: *Justice is nothing but the interest of the stronger.* At the same time another Sophist argued: *In the discussion of human affairs the question of justice only enters where there is equal power to enforce it—the powerful exact what they can, and the weak grant what they must.*

"That is heroism?" he shouted.

Others with whom he was walking glanced at him suspiciously and continued with an expression of *to-hell-with-this-newcomer* on their faces.

And the voices within him would not stop. He heard Joke's voice belching out lies in the dirty courtroom as she framed him. He also heard the voice of her lawyer as he wove his lies skilfully. At the same time, he heard the judge's voice barking out his judgment like a rabid dog, pronouncing him "Guilty!" That particular word droned on and on in his head. And then the clashing voices of Joke's relations (excluding her father's) as they walked out of the law court whispering "Congratulations" to Joke and to each other. He remembered their jubilant, hypocritical eyes staring at his tortured frame as he was being led, handcuffed, out of that dirty, vile trial room. "Oh my God!" his voice re-echoed in his head. He had wailed "Oh my God!" as piercingly as if he were condemned to death when he was sentenced. Those eyes: the eyes of the judge, the eyes of the false witnesses, the eyes of the policemen, the eyes of Joke's people, with dark patches like a goat's bile, had cast horrendous spells on him. And had he not prayed God not to hold the sin against them? Yes, he had. And those voices with those very words which had sprung up in his head like fungoid growths continued to grow.

As the prisoners came out of the hot and almost airless veranda, the zestful air of the open stirred Stephen from his reverie.

"Make una waka fast bo!" ordered Egunje, the frail-looking warder, his strident voice ringing out like a cracked bell.

"Oga, we never chop-o," retorted Grand Officer Commanding, whose title was often shortened to 'G.O.C.'

"That na true-o," added another inmate who had

the seductive eyes of a womaniser. "Man no die, man no rotten—"

"Life continues," Stephen helped him finish the popular pidgin adage.

Other prisoners trained their eyes on the new-comer who was interjecting for the second time since their journey through the long veranda. Some of them regarded him with awe; he impressed them as a bookworm. Others would not bother themselves with him.

"Oga, your nyash too flat," said one of them, directing the gazes of the others at the lean buttocks of Egunje.

"Dat na Volkswagen Igala," observed another.

"No, na *kpanla** we dey call'am."

"Dat na una bizness," said Egunje who had grown used to the prisoners' mordant humour. "After all, no be una dey help me find chick."

"Oga, so you get chick?" enthused the one with the romantic eyes of a womaniser who was nicknamed Stubborn.

"Na my wahala be dat, busybody!"

"E don damn you, Stubborn. Na'im good for you. Na so-so woman you dey wan' talk about. Na medicine dem take am do for you?"

"E concern you?" replied Stubborn angrily.

"Enough of the joke," the warder said in an authoritative manner.

"If you talk any nonsense again, Agility, I go discipline you," said Stubborn.

"Anyway, make una dey talk now. Una go see work wey no go gree una talk or sing today," the warder threatened.

The warder's words struck Stephen in a touchingly realistic way. He yawned and shuddered. He tried to imagine the fate which awaited him in the penal colony.

"Which kain work we never do as prisoners?" asked Presido, the oldest serving prisoner, as he stroked his walrus moustache. He was a middle-aged man of magnificent frame and was generally hailed as the President of the 'Republic.'

"Okay. Now una go see for una sef," answered Egunje. "After una trek go Oga Superintendent house, una go come work till una eye red like person wey smoke *igbo*."*

Stephen coughed systematically and swallowed the phlegm. The discussion was upsetting him. But what could he do?

"Dat na your own," retorted Stubborn whose

body was swollen with muscles like Michelin Man's. "After all, if e dey pain mortar e go dey pain the tin wey dem take dey pound am. Abi no bi you go escort us go there?"

"S-u-r-e, na'im now!" chorused some of the prisoners, spontaneously. Such was the spontaneity with which they composed and sang their work songs and ballads, and even embellished them with musical accompaniments produced with their work tools.

"I nor get time for una," Egunje concluded.

Meanwhile, thunder and lightning continued to rage.

The wind was whirling madly, spreading dust generously to objects around. It was snatching branches from the stems of trees and forcibly reaping immature fruits. On some of the trees, birds, seemingly ignorant of the pregnant and enervating weather, amused themselves with blissful songs. Up in the sky, an anxious cloud was scurrying westward, as if searching for bodies to pierce with arrows of rain.

While the prisoners collected their breakfast of watery beans, Stephens's past floated in his brain like the beans in the aluminium plate before him.

IT was a good number of years ago. He was still shedding his milk teeth. Olisejindu, his older and only brother, was sitting with him, watching over him. Olise was about eleven then. Their mother had died while giving birth to Stephen. She had suffered a lot of miscarriages before then. Stephen and Olise relied on their middle-aged father for sustenance. Their father had been ostracised by his own family for some obscure reasons. But one thing was suggestive: he was a very uncompromising man. With his fall from social grace, none of his immediate family related with him or his children. As Stephen and Olise sat together sharing their little world, they heard a scream, one laced with agony. Olise rushed in the direction of the scream, behind their house. At the foot of a ladder which was reclining against the wall, lay their battered father. He had accidentally fallen from the ladder. Stephen trotted to the spot. Their father's body had become clammy with sweat and his breathing weak and laboured. Olise knelt beside him. Stephen did the same. Olise raised the limp left hand of their father. It slipped from his shaky hands and slumped to the ground.

"Papa! Papa! Papa!" Stephen bellowed, perplexed by their father's plight.

"Papa's wounded. It looks like he is about to die," Olise said.

The children were confused. And Olise soon began to wail. It drew tears from the innocent Stephen.

Someone was passing by. His curiosity was aroused. He went out of his way to find out what was happening. He was temporarily shocked by the blood-chilling scene he saw. He was shaken to the bone, his adult eyes already assessing the condition of the children's father.

"Papa is—" a frightened Olise was about to explain but the lump in his throat choked his words.

The stranger swung into action. Alone, he tried to revive the unconscious man who burbled after some time, tried to shift and winced.

"Go to the next compound and fetch any grown-up," the stranger ordered Olise. As Olise left, a scared Stephen trotted after him.

They were back with a woman before spittle on a floor would dry. Acting according to the man's instructions, the woman helped the man lift the children's father into their small apartment.

One and a half years after his father's death, Olise died under mysterious circumstances. At that time,

Stephen lived with the stranger who had helped them. The man had proved to be kind. He was a tall man with athlete's foot. He was very hairy and showed it off proudly by wearing sleeveless tops. His bright, almost unblinking eyes shone with warmth and love. But he had a notorious daughter who almost made him a nervous wreck. It was this same daughter of his, Joke, who, having failed to seduce the loner, Stephen, framed him.

Misfortunes had accelerated Stephen's maturity. He had found a new world in books, especially philosophical books, and had explored all possible avenues to find books to quench his fiery thirst for knowledge, even with his tight schedule. He had read Lord Tennyson's *Ulysses* and had committed to memory the inspiring fragment:

> How dull it is to pause, to make an end,
> To rust unburnish'd, not to shine in use!
> And this grey spirit yearning in desire
> To follow knowledge, like a sinking star,
> Beyond the utmost bound of human thought.

Stephen worked as one of the packagers in a cooperative warehouse. He was fervently hoping and praying that someday he would be able to obtain the kind of *education he yearned for. Then Joke cleverly wove the web that entangled him. If only he had known. But then these circumstances of his being had conditioned his psyche. He had learnt to respond to his situation with the reflexes of someone that had grown used to solitude—physical and mental anguish. . .*

"NA riot go end this NONSENSE!" shouted a prisoner, his strident voice ripping through Stephen's reminiscence. He was looking distastefully at the fluid he had been served for breakfast.

"One day monkey go stone'im owner rotten banana. Dem go hear'am one day," said Presido.

As Stephen sat on one of the logs in a remote corner of the prison yard about to try out his meal, two flies violently whizzed past his plate. The one was chasing the other. It soon caught up with it and in a twinkle, they copulated then departed rather heartily. Stephen watched the flies in awe, pondering how ingenious the Creator was. "But is He not a witness to my misfortunes?" he reasoned. Then, he dug an aluminium spoon into the plate of beans. As he was about to scoop some into his dry mouth, he noticed a dead fly swimming in a corner of the plate.

"Commot'am now," urged Dan, an albino also known as the prison's G.O.C. Environmental. He was sitting atop a metal garbage bin, directly opposite Stephen. He had been enamoured by Stephen's seeming composure and calm disposition. From every indication, he had been craving an opportunity to establish a rapport with Stephen. Dan was a prosperous looking young man. Not only did he look remarkably wealthy, he also looked like someone who could very easily be trusted. But he had been sentenced for raping a minor.

Stephen looked at Dan suspiciously, as if he smelt mischief.

"Remove what?" Stephen asked after a brief, ominous silence in which the two prisoners sized each other up.

"Okay, pour am away," Dan dared Stephen.

Stephen yawned loudly. "And then eat what?" he retorted. Without waiting for any other suggestions from Dan, he dipped his right index finger and his thumb into the plate of beans, in the corner where the fly was, and picked it out. It appeared to have been extracted from human faeces for the meal was so bad that a dead fly looked worse for having been in it. He threw it on the ground beside Dan who crushed it beneath his fat foot and smiled, explaining:

"Ol'boy, I dey always like to crush those flies because when dem dey fly ZI-ZI-ZI for person ear or after dem shit for person food, e go be the person like say make e jus' disappear."

Stephen chuckled, nodded, then concurred:

"Yes, they can be tortuous when they mean to, and I think they always do."

As Stephen was about to shovel the third spoonful of the watery stuff into his mouth, he retched. It was the safety valve somewhere along his oesophagus that policed the escape of the vomit. He scornfully shoved the plate aside and sighed.

"Bring'am here!" Presido ordered.

Dan reluctantly passed the plate to the bulky President. He glanced at Stephen with regret.

As the prisoners ate their watery beans, they chatted, not mirthfully, but bitterly. The high point of their chat was that only a rebellion would solve such problems as the horrid food they were given to eat in the prison.

"Get set to go to the Superintendent's house where you'll be working today," announced a stern-looking senior warder. He looked like a body builder: he had pronounced chest muscles, which narrowed into a 'V' at the waistline. Beside this solidly built man was the slim warder who had been the butt of the prisoners' sarcastic humour that morning.

When the prisoners had dropped their plates, they picked up their work tools and set out for the Superintendent's residence, herded by the slim warder who had woken them up that dull morning. Getting free work done was one of the fringe benefits that the prison administrators enjoyed. It was part of what they called 'warders' enjoyment.'

It was February, that month of the year when birds take delight in cuddling and flirting to perpetuate their species. In the boughs of trees, birds, oblivious of the threatening weather, were mating. On the eastern side of the sky, a lazy sun was contesting for supremacy with thick, dark clouds. In their characteristic stubbornness, the clouds would roll over and cover the rays of the sun. But the sun, in its typical morning persistence, would insist on sending its Vitamin D-charged rays to the earth. Betwixt this dalliance of the sun and the clouds, thunder and lightning rent the sky in instalments…

"E go rain heavily today," Stubborn said. He was looking at the sky as if soliciting its approval of his observation.

"Make God do make e rain," prayed G.O.C. Environmental, glancing at Stephen.

"If it rains nko?" the warder chipped in.

"Na you go suffer'am," some of the prisoners chorused.

"You see, if e rain, e go beat your only uniform. Wetin you go come wear come work tomorrow?" asked Presido with a feeling of superiority.

"Na una e no go beat?" Egunje retorted.

"Oho! Which one concern prisoner concern—"

"Oga, a-beg give me some coins to buy cigar smoke," someone interrupted, pleading with a pedestrian for some money.

"Ol' boy, support us now," added G.O.C. Finance.

Suddenly, one of the very outspoken prisoners cued a song and all of them, except Stephen, began to sing:

Sin-ci morning I never sumoku
God go punish-i warder. . .

The warder knew better than to interrupt the

prisoners' song. When they were bored with the song they stopped and resumed cracking their ostentatious jokes.

As they walked on, Stephen cast his face down. He appeared to be counting his steps. Or to be listening to the verse-like melody his stomach was playing. It perturbed him, because it was normally a symptom of dysentery for him. He knew it, knew the chemistry of his body so well since he had not had the privilege of having a family doctor. The melody of his revolting stomach synchronised with the melody, not only of some lyrical verse, but of a lullaby. And Stephen got gradually lulled into yet another dream. . .

*I*T *was one windy Saturday morning during the harmattan. Stephen and some other prisoners were going about their routine cleaning of the precincts of the prison, especially as that day was the so-called Environmental Sanitation Day. It was the first Saturday of the month, and the military governor had set it aside for the thorough cleaning of the environment. During the period slated for the exercise, debris is hauled out*

of gutters onto roads for disposal by either government-owned vehicles, or by voluntarily donated vehicles. And during that period, citizens are not to move about freely, except those on essential services or those with permission to do so.

"The government sets a day out of about thirty days in a month for the cleaning of a nation's environment!" Stephen was amused. He looked sideways to see if anyone had heard his cynical comment. There seemed to be no one; the others were busy draining the gutter by the fence of the prison. "Initially," he continued in the same bubbling tone, "the cleaning exercise was slated to last from 7 o'clock in the morning to 12 noon. But now the time has been reduced to 10 o'clock in the morning. Who knows, next time it may be reduced to 8 o'clock, and then finally, it will be dropped." He chuckled to himself and, in his mind, congratulated the government for the weak efforts to see that the nation's environment was kept clean and, therefore, healthy. He glanced in the direction of the prison's bucket-toilet system. A sore sight confronted him: human faeces being pulverised by maggots, and flies revelling in the spot as if they had been invited to a party. Stephen shut his eyes as he always did whenever he wanted to defecate, but the mental picture was even stronger, being tinkered with, as it were, by the sinews of his inner eye.

A warder announced that the head of state was contemplating exercising his prerogative of mercy to pardon some prisoners as part of his New Year package. Some of the prisoners sprang up immediately from the ground to jubilate over their possible release in a few weeks' time. The warder's announcement made some of the prisoners' mind limber. It bedazzled Stephen's and gingered his imagination into projections for the future.

When the prisoners had finished their work for the morning, they were allowed some time to rest and then were asked to proceed to the General Hospital to clean it up.

At the hospital, Stephen met one woman who not only claimed to have been acquainted with his late mother, but also to have known him as a child.

"I learnt about how the spider spun the web that entangled you. It's the way of the world, my son. That's why we are all alone and perpetually terrified, no matter what!" The woman spoke in vernacular. "It's one of the vagaries of human nature."

"But Mama. . ." Stephen tried to speak but wasn't sure what exactly to say. He stared gloomily at the woman. She must have been quite a beautiful woman in her youth. But age and sickness had left their indeli-

ble marks on her.

"Mama," Stephen blurted out, "what's worrying you? What kind of sickness?"

"Dokinta says it's Tlaifod feva," she managed to quote her doctor, continuing in the local language: "Ehen, my son, I learnt that that girl is almost mad now, that she raves like a lunatic, drifts like a raft whose staple moorings have been loosened. I learnt that—"

"So soon?" exclaimed Stephen. "Mama, I never raped Joke. She framed me and used her connections to win the case."

"God has seen your innocence, my son. And He is avenging you. Those whom the gods want to kill, they first make mad. . ."

"WE don nearly reach *Couprintendent's** quarters." Dan's raucous voice burrowed into Stephen's daydream and roused him. "After that Psychiatric Hospital, na'im be the next compound."

The warder looked disgustedly at the prisoners, as though he was going to make a comment but decided against it.

Stephen looked up. He saw the white buildings

on the other side of the road through the barbed-wire fence. They were about eleven metres away and looked as funny as they were old. The buildings had marks of ancient architecture. Stephen developed an unusual love for the hospital. As they walked up to the hospital, he looked enchantedly at the compound.

"That is where all of us ought to be," he muttered, still sustaining his affected gaze at the hospital. He felt alone as he looked, taking in every detail. His eyes finally rested on two figures.

"Mr. Warder, na there you suppose to dey," said one of the prisoners, the one with a womaniser's eyes. He was also surveying the hospital.

Egunje maintained his silence. He looked at his wristwatch. It was almost noon. If only he had a choice, he would not be doing his present job, he thought in an exhausted moment of frankness. But he pretended to possess even more strength to trek further. He felt alone, lonely among the prisoners who continued to spin their ribald jests.

Stephen's attention was not diverted by the prisoners' rib-cracking jokes, most of which were directed at the warder and the Armed Forces which had soiled its image as a result of its unending, rapacious misrule of the nation. He remained enthralled by the two figures standing in front of one of the buildings which had inscriptions he could not decipher at that distance. They were an elderly man and a young girl. They wore the troubled looks of people who had just lost a cherished one. They looked so heavily burdened that only a heavenly rest could have relieved them. They looked so upset that one was reminded of a hen who's only surviving chick had been snatched by a merciless hawk. By their disposition, it was difficult to tell whether they were psychiatric patients themselves or not. Stephen continued to look at them as he and the other prisoners marched past the hospital. He stumbled over a little root but regained his balance. He looked sideways and noticed columns of food crops being choked by weed.

Even when the prisoners and their escort had passed the psychiatric hospital, Stephen continued to reflect on those two figures who, despite the numerous people using this hospital as a thoroughfare, were like him—as lonesome as dried-up oases in the Sahara. Perhaps it's the man's political associate, or his son, or the girl's brother, he thought. Perhaps it's the man's wife, the girl's mother. In fact, Stephen continued to reflect on how all their relations might even be in that hospital seeking one form of psychiatric aid or the other.

Everybody seemed to be going mad these days, he thought. At least to some quiet degree. Even those who were sane—that is, if there were any—could not be too sure of their own sanity. One could tell by the traffic of people into that hospital that insanity was fast shredding the fabric of people's minds, a fall-out of the disorienting regime of mad dogs under the Rock. And those two figures! Strangely isolated in a crowd, in a world thrown into confusion by all kinds of psychiatric disorders and irrationality! He chuckled as he remembered Jonathan Swift's *Ode to Reason* and Priest and Steinert's *Insanity*. Then he raised his right hand and made the sign of the Cross very mechanically.

"Una go work tire today," the warder interrupted the prisoners' piquant jests as they entered the Superintendent's compound. "Na only waka una don waka, na'im some wan' die so."

"Yeye strongman," Presido said gruffly. "No be your mates go war for Burma? You just dey dey escort people about. Wetin Fela call people like that sef? Ehm . . . ehm. . ."

"Follow-follow. Mr. Follow-follow," Stubborn helped out. Others giggled.

"Now, we go know whether Mr. Follow-follow—or wetin una wan call me again—get power or not. Bring out una file-o. Sharpen all those *langa-langa** one, two, and follow me to that side for una portions."

Some of the prisoners mumbled. But they all obeyed the warder's orders. It was as if some force in the warder's voice had propelled them. They followed him to the part of the compound to be cleared.

The compound was relatively large. Apart from a few paths, especially the one leading from the gate to the main door of the otherwise beautiful house, the compound was overgrown with grass. The celibate Superintendent was not known to bother about cleanliness. One could tell this from his usually shabby appearance. Besides the dirty uniform, he usually wore a T-shirt the colour of the tail of a few days old wall gecko over a rusty brown pair of trousers. Whenever he was reproved for his scruffiness by his outspoken friends, he would feebly defend himself either by saying that it was because he lived alone and hardly had time for such things, or that it was in his nature. "You're the way you are," he would say.

After Egunje had farmed out portions to the prisoners, they began to work. Much of the grass was of the stubborn type; as stubborn as the gloomy clouds that had refused to submit to the sun's incipient dominance of the sky. The more experienced prisoners skilfully sliced them down. Stephen painfully struggled to cut the ones in his portion with the blunt cutlass he had been given.

Approximately halfway into their portions, Dan suggested that they should relax to recoup lost energy. They all agreed and made for the shade below an umbrella tree. They had hardly sat down than they began to throw highly-charged lewd jokes at the warder.

"I hear say your blokoss no dey rise again," said Stubborn, referring to the rumoured impotence of the warder. "Dem say na so-so hand you dey use. Ah, the fingering practice Bala spoke of!"

"Nonsense! If only you for give me your sister for experiment . . ."

"Dat na true," said a prisoner with a shrill voice. He looked like a ghost out of a cemetery.

"Oya now," some of them urged the warder.

Stephen kept calm all this while. He was tactfully examining the blisters that had appeared on his right palm. He was thinking that if this was how the rest of his days in the penal colony would be then death was preferable. Of course, I am right at the end of my life, he mused. I should be dying like a setting sun to escape this lonely, agonising, unjust existence. He tried harder to meditate upon that metaphysical concept DEATH, but he didn't seem to be uncovering anything new. The more he thought about it, the more confused he became. He felt his bottom aching. He stood up and straightened his body. His bones creaked. He felt a stab of pain on his forehead. He looked at the sky, towards the region where it seemed to merge with the earth. It struck him that it was quite an expectant sky, with a womb laden with monstrous anger. A stream of breeze wafted the stench from the Superintendent's room to the relaxing prisoners. It assaulted Stephen's olfactory sense. It benumbed his brain.

"Shit!" he blurted out.

"Na so warders' nyash dey smell," Stubborn said, glaring menacingly in the warder's direction.

"Abi no be so, Oga Egunje?"

"Dat's your business, talkative." The warder's voice was firm and his manner became brisk. "Everybody, stand up make una go back to work. Day don dey go!" He took a long look at his wristwatch.

"People wey no dey used to watch, na so dem dey count the minutes before dem know the time," said someone.

They all giggled.

"It's almost three, and na only half una don work. People like Oyibo never even work reach halfway. Na so e go dey do like palm oil wey dey sleep."

They all giggled again, glancing askance at Dan to whom the warder had directed his tease.

"Una no get sense," Stubborn said, "otherwise una for no dey laugh for the *okpata** wey korofo dey yarn."

They laughed even more as they all rose reluctantly from the soothing ground. Just above their heads, between the twigs of the shady tree, birds were chirping soulfully. As if in response to the incantatory songs of the birds, one of the prisoners, the one with a shrill, tinny voice, burst into a song.

Aside Stephen and two others who were still

unfamiliar with the songs and the prisoners' culture, everyone else joined in. Thus, as they shuffled to their portions, they sang:

Worku worku kere'le o
Wina wina kere'le o
Worku worku here we come o
Wina wina coming o . . .

As they sang the work song, some of them accompanied it with the striking of cudgels serving as musical instruments. The blend was near-professional. It was so captivating that even the Superintendent who was known for his lack of interest in music peeped out of his window to see the prisoners-turned-musicians.

Meanwhile, that opprobrious rotten-egg smell wafting out of the Superintendent's room had extinguished Stephen's consciousness and transported him back in time.

HE *was living as a houseboy with a rich man in a city. The man had two Alsatian dogs. Before he enlisted*

the services of Stephen, he used to feed the dogs heavily by himself. But with Stephen's arrival, he entrusted the feeding of his beloved wolves to Stephen, who himself was not being properly fed. The man, a misanthrope, usually measured Stephen's food. And, so, Stephen lived with an omnipresent hunger. To tackle the crushing hunger, he began to eat part of the dogs' food. One day, he ate so much of the dogs' share that he was compelled to adulterate the dogs' soup with water. The 'strange soup' was so tasteless that the dogs, even in their hunger, would not eat it. Mounting hunger provoked the dogs. Their owner was out and Stephen's petting would not assuage their anger. They charged at him. He ran for dear life. Along the road, a slatternly dressed young girl, unconscious of the danger, was strolling by. Stephen breezed past her. She opened her mouth to curse him. Then the dogs came snarling at her . . .

A pellet of rain stabbed Stephen on his pate and restored his consciousness. He looked around half-dreamily. He noticed that rain was dropping haphazardly and that his colleagues had stopped singing. They had pounced on their portions, the spasmodic drops of rain notwithstanding.

"Make this rain fall-o," said Oyibo.

"Whether it falls or not, una must finish una portion. Dat na the order from Comptroller General." The supervising warder's words, coupled with the hunger brewing in Stephen, caused his intestines to churn. He bit his lips and continued to endure like the rest.

Stubborn broke into another song:

Warder get belle-ooo . . .

Others spontaneously chorused:

E go born am today-ooo . . .

The rain began to pour down from the sky in earnest.

"No movement! Orders is orders. Mind una portions," the warder commanded, watching the rain bespattering the helpless prisoners, who, as though possessed by the god of obedience, obliged.

The rain continued to drone. It shot its arrows gloomily at the working, defenceless prisoners. Its torrents thumped on the rooftops and on the hungry prisoners with the rhythm of violence. The sky belched thunderously. It continued to roar as if it were doomsday; as if it had something to gain, or this were a mere game, the sky continued to send out its darts of rain to pierce the working prisoners. The rain fell in a frenzy, sounding like a monotonous dirge. It stomped the prisoners as if in an attempt to stave them into the earth. Sporadic flashes of lightning dazzled them as the arrows continued to fall. And as if the rain had induced them into subservience, the prisoners kept on working under the deluge. Or perhaps it was some obscure god of peace that had dispossessed them of their rebellious, outspoken spirit. Even as their strength continued to wane, they kept on working.

Glued to the stem of the umbrella tree, the warder watched the pathetic sight. Their portions were almost finished. And the rain's shafts continued to stab away at them. Occasionally Steven would clench his left fist, while his blistered right palm clutched the blunt cutlass absent-mindedly.

By some rare coincidence, the rain stopped abruptly as the last of the prisoners finished cutting his remaining square of over-grown grass.

"Thanks be to God," said Stephen, more to himself, as they marched moodily out of the compound.

The prisoners, followed by the warder, shuffled solemnly into the prison yard that sombre evening. A chilly wind assailed them in their wet khaki uniforms, throwing them into a somnolent mood. And they were still hungry and hollow within.

Their journey from the Superintendent's house had been quite uninteresting. They'd maintained a grave silence most of the time. When some of them talked at all, it had revolved around mordant matters: What would they eat? How would it be? What would happen when they got to the prison? Would there be a fulfilment of the bloody rumour that had been smouldering within the past two days?

As they went into the premises, Stephen's attention was attracted by two lizards running along the massive fence of the prison. The one was after the other in a deathly chase. Soon they disappeared around the edge of the wall. Stephen tried to ponder all those caustic whispers about an impending bloody action. But he could not think properly. His stomach continued to grumble from hunger. At times it would even growl, as if insisting on being listened to.

Once inside the prison compound, the sight of the kitchen seemed to restore energy to the prisoners. But there was no aroma in the air. The air was still. Only the first chirpings of night insects abused the stillness. Somewhere, among the trees in the prison yard, a big black bird with a yellow beak was hooting as it pleased. But none of the prisoners seemed to be conscious of these sounds announcing the close of the day. Only the kitchen mattered now. And they were headed there with great expectation.

"Man go wack and die this evening," announced Presido.

"Dat na sure-banker," said Stubborn, scratching his abdomen, his eyes dilating owlishly.

"Dis kain hunger sef!" Oyibo remarked.

"Dis kain tiredness sef!" said another. He was an emaciated and ageing man.

Somebody hissed like an angry snake.

"Unbearable!" Stephen exclaimed matter-of-factly.

"No food NOW!" announced a fierce-looking, ugly warder as the prisoners built a wall in front of the kitchen door.

"No what?" The chorus was hysterical.

"Easy!" the warder continued. "The prison authorities have decided to shift your dinner time from five p.m. to eight p.m."

An ominous silence succeeded the words of the ugly warder, during which, it seemed, the prisoners were trying to understand what he had said. The information seeped into them, stirring their bowels with anguish. They stood still as if in meditation. Or, as if they were undergoing some transfiguration, some deathly transfiguration. Some of the prisoners trembled as if the earth shook beneath them. Stephen yawned loudly. Another prisoner yawned loudly. And yet another. A light-skinned, stockily-built warder appeared on the scene. He was followed by two more weird-looking warders.

"Excuse me," an enlightened prisoner spoke up. "What is our connection with all these endless excuses you and your cohorts keep on offering for our triangular—mind you, not square—meals? The other day it was that the authorities could no longer cope with the astronomical cost of garri and therefore . . . bla-bla-bla . . . Today, it's that the authorities have decided to change dinner time. What will it be tomorrow? The authorities can no longer sustain the cost of feeding us? Do you really know what hunger is like?"

As if in answer to the question, one of the prisoners staggered forward hungrily and slumped to the wet ground, like Goliath, defeated.

"I have told you to go until eight p.m. Don't stay here running diarrhoea of the mouth like people who have not eaten since yester—"

A hefty prisoner in the front row dazed the ugly warder with a slap which resounded like a harsh jazz instrument. The prisoner's action galvanised the others. They went on the rampage.

Stubborn went for the stockily-built warder's throat. He clung stubbornly to it, squeezing it with all of a hungry man's might and wrath. Stephen, as if propelled by some unseen force, dived at one of the insensitive warders. Another prisoner also went for the warder Stephen had attacked. When Stephen saw that the other prisoner had clung to the warder's scrotum, squeezing them like grapes, he let go. Somebody had sent his fingers into one of the bulging, brown eyes of yet another warder. When he withdrew his fingers, the warder's blood-drenched, one-eyed face looked like that of a victim of Dracula.

There was pandemonium.

The prisoners dashed into the kitchen. They attacked the cooks, leaving only their inmates who had been deployed to help in the kitchen. They beat up the kitchen staff mercilessly, seizing whatever they laid their hands on. Some grabbed raw tomatoes, some bottles of oil, and others, plates of *eba*. They ate ravenously.

They left the kitchen with the stuff they could not eat and went in search of their inmates who had gone to the prison offices. Only a few warders were found there. They brought them out and *drummed* them mercilessly. Some of the warders who were still conscious after the beatings, escaped for their lives. The prisoners stripped the fallen warders. Some tore the warders' uniforms. Some hid the uniforms. Some played frisbee with the warders' caps.

It started to drizzle with the arrival of armed policemen from a nearby station. They had been tipped off. The policemen arrived and swung into action, shouting orders, shoving with gun butts, and emptying teargas canisters to dispel the rioting prisoners who retreated into their cells, lucky that none fell to the Force's infamous 'accidentally-discharged' bullets.

STEPHEN was so harried by the previous day's riot that he slipped into a tortuous meditation about how it had been executed and quelled like the flashes of lightning that had startled earlier that day. But he could not sustain his meditation. He shifted his foot nervously. His head throbbed as if a blacksmith were working in there. The alacrity with which they had handled the warders confused his thinking. He could not understand how the hefty prisoner had managed to pluck the raw nerve of their collective rage. Just one hungry man's disturbing fall, and it had sparked off a chain of reactions. It had loosened the knots in their heads and freed the wild fowl of violence imprisoned in their minds. He yawned loudly and quickly rebuked himself for almost waking his fellow inmates who were still snoring beside him. He rose from the creaking bed, regarded his fellow inmates and the cell for a while, then trudged to the hole that constituted the window.

Through the hole he peered outside. The brightness outside almost blinded him. He shut his eyes. After a few seconds that seemed like centuries, he opened them. He saw a whirlwind in the prison compound. The wind was swirling madly, sweeping dust generously and spraying it carelessly on the surrounding objects in the same manner as some filthily rich Nigerians spray money like confetti on favoured dancers. The wind spun speedily, ascending with the whirling objects like some rider to apocalypse. As it spun while Stephen watched, it seemed to melt his consciousness. Once, or twice, he seemed to drift into a trance. He tried to compare the previous night's events to the whirling wind but lacked sufficient concentration to do so. He yawned again. The rancid smell from his own mouth surprised him.

"What the hell is—" A scream from one of the inmates who was experiencing a nightmare interrupted him. "I wish I had the room to myself as I did yesterday," he muttered. Then he heard shouts of protest coming from a few cells away, somewhere in the wing for condemned prisoners now reserved for human-rights and pro-democracy activists whose arrests and indefinite detention without trial, General Babayaro, the dictatorial Head of State, ordered at will. Often after tagging them 'dangerous extremists.'

The shouts, jumbled but vehement, had a ring of hysteria: "Una no go do am o. No, no be for this cell. We don tire. E no go happen! Never! Killers! Criminals! Get away! Who kill una for the tief wey una dey tief? All of una na tief! Because nobody catch una and una oga? Authority tiefs! Authority stealing pass armed robbery. Leave am-oo. . ."

"Na we condemn am to death? We just dey obey the law. Obedience is the first law in heaven," a warder countered the babble of the inmates of the cell.

In that cell, two armed policemen and a warder were busy trying to take a condemned man away.

The riotous protest of his fellow inmates roused other prisoners who had been sleeping. In the prison yard, an Assistant Superintendent of Police, some Local Government officials who were to supervise the execution, and a truck loaded with armed policemen, waited impatiently. And the protesting voices continued to rise, ascending to a crescendo:

"NO WAY. NO, NEVER. NOT AGAIN. ENOUGH IS ENOUGH. NA TODAY E GO END. ALL OF US GO DIE JOIN. ALL OF US GO QUENCH HERE. . ."

Like an epidemic, the charged voices of the pro-

testers infected the other prisoners with an out-
burst of fury. It was as if the prisoners' anger of the
previous night was yet to dissipate. With the fury
of charging bulls, some of the prisoners who were
already out and working in the precincts began to
destroy everything in sight in an unusual show of
strength. They seemed to be possessed by some
savage demons. And like furious waves rolling
toward a busy shore, they surged towards the
cell from where the shouts emanated.

"Nobody go touch the man!" ordered one of the
prisoners. His eyeballs swam with rage. "That man
is a good old man."

"Yes! Yes! Yes-s!" chorused the rest.

"We say NO to execution!"

"NO to firing squad!"

"NO to HUNGER!"

The officials sensed that rebellion was afoot.
Without hesitation they hustled militarily into the
dingy veranda which led to the cells. The glowing
electric bulbs lit the way.

"NO NONSENSE or I'll order the police to
shoot!" thundered the Assistant Superintendent of
Police, his voice reverberating with anxiety.

"Shoot animals?"

Stubborn's words ignited the others. Some pounced on the executioners. Others took care of the remaining policemen, warders, and the Local Government officials. The prisoners used the rods they had wrested from their cells' barricades. They swung them freely. There was chaos. The Superintendent's head was ripped open. His pulpy brain spilled out. The policemen started to shoot randomly at the prisoners. The gunshots invited other policemen in the neighbourhood barracks. They advanced toward the prison yard in five vehicles. They were led by an Assistant Commissioner in charge of operations, and were armed with teargas canisters, batons and guns. Their arrival escalated the riot, forcing some of the prisoners to seek escape routes, while others retreated into their cells, prepared to leave the fight for another day.

The escaping prisoners ran towards the exit at the end of the veranda, striding through a bath of blood. Stephen was among those rushing to the exit. The reinforcement of the policemen had increased their steam and firepower. With renewed gusto, they continued to squeeze their triggers, shattering the limbs of the unlucky escapees. A bullet caught

Stephen on the side of his chest, ripped through his flesh, shattered his ribs, and lodged in his heart. He staggered out of the veranda, his heart pumping pain to the rest of his own body. He collapsed on the cold ground. But the cold ground would not soothe his burning body. He swooned from overpowering pain. And his own heart continued to pump away his blood.

"Lord, receive my spirit," he prayed. Then he visualised his outpouring blood congealing into a thread linking his ebbing life with death, while his deathly life spun around the bloody thread like a whirlwind strung together at the centre by an invisible force. He also saw his soul escaping from his pain-tanned body and ascending into a horizon lit by the moon and stars, heralded by the symphonic music of freedom.

Three ambulances and a *Black Maria* arrived at the scene. Some policemen and warders marched the captured prisoners into the waiting vans for transfer to Kirikiri Maximum Security Prison. Others, including the health workers, walking across the 'Second Golgotha,' lifted victims of the rebellion into the ambulances.

Stephen lay supine in one of the over-used

ambulances. The old Peugeot 504 station wagon was ostensibly racing to the General Hospital on the outskirts of town. He lay there like a hollow bone still being scoured by the greedy dog called pain. And his tired and lacerated heart ticked away like a clock about to stop because its cellular life was almost spent.

Jubilant Flames

*Like withered grass the
minds of men catch fire.*

— Holderlin

*Underlying the poetry of this
surrender is the one long and
huge irony of endurance.*

— Es'kia Mphahlele

ODIES! *Everywhere, bodies! This trampling, that crumpling. This elbowing, that cursing. Among these bodies, at a vantage position, stand I. My teeth chattering, my fists clenched, my scared eyes glued to the centre. At the centre of this crowd, a wild inferno, its hungry flames leaping up with agony and joy as it roasts some animal. The acrid smell of roasting meat clashes with the rancid odour emitting from our bodies, like consonants within a stammerer's utterance . . . And the heifer keeps burning! Its eyes pop, its tissues crackle, its flesh tears . . . And the issuing fluid disappears into the fire and the ashes . . . and hisses! The crowd yells hysterically like customers of a sort waiting for Mallam's suya to grill at the so-called University of Suya, Faculty of Meatology, Allen Campus. . .*

"Kika! Kika . . . Kikachukwu!" Uduak, one of my neighbours, a short sixteen-year-old girl, rescued me from the horrid sight of the charred remains of a human body.

"Kika, I just asked you to tell me that story about the cobbler's death. And then you suddenly went blank, or as Eno would say, you blacked out. I hope—"

"O Chukwu! The scene was an open oven! Uduak, I wish one could never recall that hellish sight again. Whatever made Suleiman—that handsome, clowning cobbler, ever smiling, ever making his clients laugh—let go…! Well, forget it."

"But you promised to let me hear from . . . ehm, the horse's mouth," Uduak reminded me. She held my right wrist in her palms, which were rough like those of a hewer, imploring me with a tortured gaze.

"You don't understand, Uduak. I'm getting sick of narrating the shocking story over and over."

"Even to me? I haven't heard the exact gist. Just

fragments of hearsay. Please!"

"And each time, even now, as you just witnessed, my mind boggles at the disturbing idea of . . . you know?" I cleared the lump from my throat, motioning for Uduak to sit on the rotting stump beside her mother's *buka*.* "I can make do with standing."

"Oh, thanks, Brother Kika," she enthused. "Thanks. I'll never disturb you again after this."

"Oho, it's only now you're respecting the seven years age difference between us. I don't even give a damn, you know?"

"Oh, I'm sorry. I didn't mean to—"

"But what does it matter? What does it remove from me?"

"Oh, it's all right then. I'm sorry. Okay, the story." Uduak's voice, tremulous with impatience, struck me.

"Okay, listen attentively. Remember, I'll not repeat any words, talk less of repeating the story. So, open your ears."

Uduak shifted into a more comfortable sitting position.

"I gave Suleiman that my *waka-about** pair of black shoes to work on the eroded soles."

Uduak smiled.

"Of course, you know they have borne the brunt of my endless hunt for stories to write as a free-lance journalist! That was on the other day Local Government officials and some Mobile Policemen raided those traders again—"

"Oh, the so-called hawkers!" Uduak interrupted, steering her big head in the direction of an arriving figure.

It was her friend Eno whose beauty always distracted me. I purposely allowed plenty of time for the friends to exchange greetings and remarks and adjust to suitable sitting positions and the right listening mood. And those were luxuries I seldom allowed whenever I told people stories. But she really had to be excepted, to fully appreciate the lustre, the fullness, the provocation of her well-sculpted physique.

"Ehen, Brother Kika..." Uduak intruded on my self-indulgence.

"Okay, as I was saying, that was the day those whatever-they call-them . . . were raided at Oshodi—"

"Eno, stop disturbing me," I heard Uduak warn in a near-whisper. Listen!"

"The traders scampered with their wares into the

maddening crowd milling around the bus stop and the railway line, the so-called Illegal Market. When the officials had gone, the traders, the artisans, returned to their businesses. Suleiman returned to his favourite position. Shay you know the place? He returned, smouldering with anger. He lost his radiant smile as he had lost one of his needles in the stampede. Suleiman lost his humour. Instead, he found a torrent of complaints. And his Hausa could never have been more poetic, never more fluent!"

"So you understand Hausa too?" Eno asked.

"He's a real *Wazobia,* having spent his infancy in the North, his adolescence here in the West, and being an Igbo chap . . . But would you for once seal those ever-leaking lips of yours?" Uduak shot another warning look at Eno. "Ehen . . . Brother Kika! Don't mind her," she prompted once more, searching out, as it were, my straying, lustful gaze.

"And Suleiman spoke rapidly about all those misfortunes that were written all over the pages of his life: how he had been born a few weeks after his father's death; how his only two brothers had died in a motor accident; how his mother had died after being delivered of a stillborn child; how his only sister now prostituted herself; how he had lost his job as a night watchman; how he had taken to shining and mending shoes—an art he claimed was second nature to him; how 'gofment' would not let him and other *talakawas** earn the coins to survive; how . . . my God! I can't remember all.

"Hey, girls, you need to have seen the sparks in his eyes! They darted arrows of ehm . . . ehm . . . you know?

"But he shone with his sunny smile afterwards, when his anger, his disappointments, his misfortunes . . . when he had poured them forth."

"Oh, the last incident," Uduak cued impatiently. "I don't have the whole day to myself. I've got to help Mama with the service. Brother Kika, the real action, please."

"Let him land now," Eno cautioned her.

"Yes, I'm coming," I assured, looking towards Uduak's mother's *buka*. Dusk was closing in and business was just opening. It was rush hour. Soon, People's Buka would be alive with men eager to appease their growling stomachs, eager to lubricate their parched throats.

I understood.

"Okay," I continued, "that other day . . . four days

ago . . . I mean that afternoon that it looked like the sun was to suffer an eclipse, that day before the papers reported the sighting of Halley's Comet . . . Yes, that day. I went to Business Line to collect those my pair of shoes as appointed . . ."

Eno eyed me questioningly. Oh, how I liked those lovely, dreamy, seductive eyes! But what didn't I like about her, anyway? Having surrendered to her beauty, I shifted my weight to the other leg. Uduak's less than five-foot-five, rather masculine frame wore the cloak of understanding.

"As I was inspecting my shoes that day, those nitwits swooped down like eagles for yet another raid. But am I the harbinger of ignoble raids? This time, the *green khaki boys** were with them. Stampede! The coconut heads were lashing, slapping, booting, looting. Confusion! They were pillaging, raiding the traders' wares: second-hand books, *okiri-ka** clothes, foodstuff. Everything, including young girls' supple breasts, God! The pack of hoodlums had set up a bonfire on the garbage heap by the railway line. The traders, O God! The artisans, the young chaps—poor destitute children of a second-hand generation. They all ran, some of them luckily escaping with their belongings and with only bruises. Pandemonium! Hell! Yes, it was Hell. It was as if a mad dog had entered a henhouse. And the law enforcement agents kept on enforcing their raid. The foodstuff in their vehicles, they happily cast the other items into the fire in a manner that reminded one of Fela's lyrics: "Na the burn-burn, na'im dey sweet dem pass. . ." Every time a set of items was thrown in, the fire jubilated, crackling endlessly. . .

"Into the inferno were thrown poor Suleiman's survival tools and things. Into the bonfire were thrown the jewels they dispossessed the wretched man of—his needles and nails!

"And one of those satanic messengers compensated Suleiman with a dirty slap, echoes of which resound in my ears even now. Stripped, dehumanised, Suleiman spat into the sultry atmosphere. His spittle missed the zombie it was aimed at narrowly. *Chineke!** If you saw the daggers in his fiery coals of eyes! Sunken in his gloomy face, they glittered in their sockets.

"*Olorun o ma she-o.** If you saw Suleiman's six-foot-plus frame shrink! God! Stripped! Slapped by a military boy about seven years younger than him! Dehumanised! His cherished possessions thrown into hungry flames by uniformed people bereft of any iota of reasoning! Dispossessed! *Wallahi!** Suleiman shrunk to a shadow. And nobody took notice of him. A ghost in a cemetery! But I did see the ghost. I did see it, saw the living-dead man. I saw everything through my misty eyes, through the smoke-filled air. But I could not help. How could an unarmed chick stop the eagle armed with its extended talons from carrying off its sister chick? We were all helpless."

The scene replaying itself in slow motion inundated my mind with disgust. No, anguish! Or was it…? I wasn't quite sure what.

"Lord! I saw the apparition of my shrunken, dispossessed, sad cobbler friend. But it was too late. And others saw him when it was too late, too …

"But he wasn't the only unlucky artisan. I can't understand! He was too shaken—must have been shaken to the very roots of his pubic hairs! Stripped. But he hadn't lost all. He still had his own blood coursing through his own weary veins. He should have known. He had his life. But was it really too late? Were we really helpless? If I had known! But I knew! Eno, I knew! I couldn't fight armed men with my bare hands. But I should have stopped Suleiman. He might have listened if I had called to him. And his mind may not have completely unhinged. He might have realised he still had . . . ehm . . . is it friends, or what now? Admirers? But how was I to be sure of the construction on his mind? But even if I was sure of it, didn't someone once suggest that *to save a man against his will is as bad as to murder him?*

"And he lost control. Suleiman let go! He surrendered! That was when the crowd saw him."

I felt the roughness around my wrist. But then I felt something rougher: the surrender in the fiery coals of Suleiman's eyes burning with disgust for a blighted world as he spat into the sultry atmosphere set my mental eye ablaze. It seemed he meant that there wasn't time to say goodbye before joining his possessions in those joyous flames that grievously relieved him of the burden of survival.

"Oh, I should have known! Lord! We should have known! Kikachukwu should have known! Oh, Suleiman! The rest of the world saw you then. Rather too late. When you let go and followed your possessions to eternity. That was when the people gathered to see you—a spectacle! Never before, in your lifetime, had such a crowd gathered round you. But then what else would you have wanted them to do, Suleiman? They were there, looking at their own lives in flames exploding with eternal canons at the most mournful funeral of our time."

Lost in thought, I felt icy balls of tears tumble out of my weary eyes. All they were seeing were *bodies . . . fire . . . the yelling crowd . . . fire melting flesh and bones. . .*

THEN, a nudge accompanied with some words I didn't quite get . . . I mopped my eyes and my forehead with a handkerchief. I looked sideways: Eno and Uduak were by my flanks. The latter's rough palms were around my wrist. Embarrassed by their silence, I wasn't quite sure what next to say.

"Sorry, I . . . ehm . . . got so e-motional," I stuttered with grief.

"Oh, it's okay, Brother Kika," Uduak responded.

"Thanks so much," Eno's mellifluous voice sang. "We're very grateful. We now know what really happened."

"Eno, how would you compare what we just

heard with the one we heard at Agege yesterday? Hmm . . . hearsay! Oh, may Suleiman's soul rest in perfect peace!"

"Amen," Eno and I chorused.

"Let's go over to the shop," Uduak whispered.

As we strolled to People's Buka, Eno's body brushed past mine. *Wallahi!* My veins went asunder with lust, making me uncomfortable around the groin. I looked at her but couldn't see much of her beauty. The steely potency of darkness overpowering the last rays of the day's light had consumed it as the jubilant flames had consumed Suleiman and his belongings.

Wings of Rebellion
(Song of Liberation)

*We live here for the most in an
oral world whose
daily organisation is ruled by
the written word.*

— Chenjerai Hove

"Our tale is a bride

waiting

For the nimble fancy of the growing ear."

AH! Nduka, I know those lines. They're from Niyi Osundare's Waiting Laughters *and I am sure you've chosen them to remind me yet again of the tale, that tale you've been bothering me to tell you. Ah! Those lines really touched the right chord. It touched me inside—if I may confess without fear of your attributing to manya* the increasing traffic of words from my mouth when you mentioned at our last drinking bout that I've got to expose my tales. In your words, they, being manifestations of our incoherent lives, would be of some use to the public.*

Yes, Nduka, you were right. May I then invite your honourable poetic self to share in the minutest details of this intriguing tale entitled Wings of Rebellion?

Oh, that title beats your imagination? Well, please, my good friend, the noble poet, may I warn that you'll make me uneasy reminding me of your poetic sensibilities, and, therefore, make me have to hammer out this tale to satisfy them—poetic sensibilities are often stubbornly arrogant and difficult to satisfy.

Oh, you are sorry! Keep your apology, please. Is it not the same 'aloof poetic sensibility' that spurred the Okigbos to preclude non-poets from their poetic fellowships? Is it not that strain of transcendental 'madness' that makes some poets enjoy a riotous lifestyle? Is it not what made the wise Plato to champion their banishment from the Republic? Is it not. . .

Now you're getting angry and impatient. How impatient poets can be! Eh-hen? You're laughing at that? If you knew how mischievous that glint of wine in your eyes sparkles when you laugh . . . Well, here goes the tale. But first, promise me another bottle of Guinness for the journey … Good! … And would you mind filling my glass for me to warm me up for the journey? Oh lovely! What a kind poet laureate we have. . .

Ah, that track of Fela's is relevant to our journey. Nduka, listen: "Woman na mattress," sings the maverick Afrobeat King:

FELA:	Call am for me, call am for me
CHORUS:	Mattress, mattress
FELA:	Call am for me, call am for me
CHORUS:	Mattress, mattress
FELA:	It is the one wey we dey sleep on top, call am for me
CHORUS:	Mattress, mattress
FELA:	If e be mat wey e dey cold for ground
CHORUS:	Mattress, mattress
FELA:	If e be plank wey e dey hard for back
CHORUS:	Mattress, mattress
FELA:	If e be spring wey e dey bounce like ball
CHORUS:	Mattress, mattress
FELA:	If e be cushion wey e dey soft like wool
CHORUS:	Mattress, mattress
FELA:	E be mat, e be plank, e be spring, e be cushion
CHORUS:	Mattress, mattress...

Ha! ha! ha! ha! Thanks for the music, barman. But please go and switch it off. Our tale is about to take wings . . . Aha! This my bearded friend here is Soyinka. Ever met him before?

What did you say? "Good evening, Mister Soyinka the dictionary himself"? LAUGHTER.

Ehe! There, the wrinkles come again spreading on his forehead like ripples! And his eyes blinking like an owl's. . .

Haba! Nduka! Don't be too insolent. Twenty-seven-year-olds are not supposed to be. And you, barman, tender an apology and withdraw the "Mister". Don't you know, as Nduka my poetic friend always insists, writers' names are richer without prefixes?

Now, better. All right, forgive him, Dambudzo. Enough of the bickering.

Thank you very much. I've heard you. I'll stop playing the . . . what does Fela call it again? Ehm . . . 'Original Perambulator'!

Now, I hope the tape is still rolling. I'm not sure I'll be able to tell this tale a second time. Even If I succeed, remember that every 'telling' is unique in its own way. . .

Did I hear you say you want to erase the foregoing preamble? No, Eliot! Leave the whole job to me. I'll do the transcription and then faithfully edit the text to suit my style. That is, put it the way I want it published. This is not verse. It is an extended prose-poem. Okay? All right then. I'll go ahead, straightaway. Lend me your attention...

ONCE upon a Sunday in July—that month in the season of rains which has inspired many a poet to unusual lyricism—the thunder was, with its accomplice, lightning, rending the sky like rockets. And the world was draped in little showers of rainfall, deviant slants of rainwater. The rain's soft drops on the rooftop thrilled the ears in the same way the songs of weaverbirds warbling up in the safety of their nests would.

It was morning yet on the Sunday. It was dawn —that last lap of nightfall when, normally, humanity is at the nadir of pleasurable sleep. Yes, it was dawn —that first segment of a day when the last crows of the cock warn the sun to begin its diurnal pilgrimage, to begin its secret daily manoeuvres that overthrow the late morning moon and its retinue of stars.

In Suite 1013 of Ariya Hotel in Iduu, a moderately-built, middle-aged man with a mortar-like bald head and a pair of eyes that popped out like those of a rat caught in an *mkpakala** was astride a whore's axle. He was astir like the rain showers, riding towards orgasm. He was riding so fast, as all whore patrons do just before dawn, trying to ride to their satisfaction before the expiration of their fees at the first stab of daylight. Soon, he donated that stuff which men donate to women in such circumstances, slid from her body and lay on the bed panting like Randy Rudy the dog.

LAUGHTER . . . My friend, I can see your pestle pounding beneath you. Calm down, and remember that it has been the undoing of many a man. If I had enough courage, I'd have cut off mine. For, as my paternal grandfather used to say, for all the restlessness and pride your man boasts of, no sooner does he set to prove himself than he pisses in the house and withdraws in shame. LAUGHTER.

Keep laughing! You might as well be laughing at yourself as you're laughing at our man.

Aha. He lay by his harlot, exhausted. It had been a long night, you know. Our man, Akaaga son of Uzi, son of Anyibuofu, was sprawled on the bed like a woman in labour. But his whore was still agile. She had risen from the bed, strolled towards the pair of red curtains by the head of the bed. She parted the curtain mid-length—the curtain was hung on a box just above the window and flowed to the floor like Mammy Wata's hair. As the whore parted the curtain, a stream of infant daylight greeted her half-naked body. That same stream of young daylight also greeted Akaaga's *opolo** eyes. He responded with a tired grunt and changed his position. He buried his head in the pillow. But it was not that Akaaga was feeling anything near some teenager's coyness. Ah! He had seen many a whore's undies. In fact, it was experience that had introduced him to the epitome, to the Amazon of those commercial sex workers—apologies to feminists—Sandra. And was it not his performance that once made a lady describe him as being as good as a professional pornographic film actor?

O Nduka, beware of Sandra whose delicate beauty, 'half education' and professional antics won her the presidency of the illegal PEPLEPPA . . .

Now, don't begin to interject questions for simple abbreviations like that. After all, it was the plunge that a member of the People Pleasing People with Pleasure Association allowed a member of your vocation that sent him to nirvana . . .

Ehm . . . Sandra! She was a marvel to behold. What drove her into that Association will make another story. But she had been partly guided by her heroine Ramatou's words: "The world made a whore of me; I want to turn the whole world into a whorehouse" . . . Ever seen the goddess of beauty? Sandra was the goddess incarnate!

Meanwhile, Nduka, watch the bottle. We're nearing the bottom and our tale is just beginning to unfold . . .

Aha! If you saw Sandra nude! No, even half-dressed as she was that Sunday morning—a wrapper tied around her chest like Mama Bomboy's—looking at the world through the glass window upon which her breath shot vapours. . .

Endee, hope you're following?

Gosh! Sandra was a figurative expression: a metaphor. She was a metaphor of physical beauty. For, although in her early thirties, her breasts still hung firmly with the pointed arrogance of a teenager's. Her oval face was delicately punctuated, with a bewitching pair of bird-of-prey eyes and an average-sized pair of naturally red lips which contorted slightly, became taut and pouted simultaneously, as if pining for a kiss, whenever she smiled. Her pair of conspicuous dimples beautified her face whenever she smiled. Her proportionately extraordinary 'I' trunk metamorphosed into a groovy 'C' at her midriff. The outer curve of the 'C' midriff in turn metamorphosed into an attractive 'B' pair of buttocks, big enough to make it difficult for a baby strapped to her back to slide down. Oh, how ingenious the Creator is! Her dark complexion, the very colour of the night itself, shone with the pride of a polished ebony surface. But even with the shine of her skin, it would have been difficult to outline her shape and that of the coffee-complexioned Akaaga as they had entwined. Surprisingly, she hadn't bleached her skin as did most members of her Association. She could well have taken a sauna bath, but she hadn't. She, only she, Sandra, knew the secret of her beautiful skin.

Her legs were like Akaaga's: long and sturdy like the elephant's. But they never bothered her, never made her self-confidence to waver. Soon, she began to write playfully the balance of her fee on the misty glass. She hardly would complete writing it before it would vanish like letters on a magic slate. She was delighted by the appearance and disappearance of the letters. She likened it to the phenomenon of dreaming; likened it to the notion of reality and fantasy; likened it to the other possibilities of substance and shadow.

And time stealthily stole away as she waited rather too patiently for Akaaga to settle the fee. No doubt, from the look of comprehensive satisfaction she had glimpsed on his face, she had more than fed his pleasure, far more than his wife—even more than any of her colleagues—would have. In fact, she was expecting some *jara** from her client. She had given him hers. . .

"Of course, the barman knows his strategies too. He has to add our own jara later."

Have you heard that? Ah? That last speaker is the Dean of the Faculty of Alcohol and we are his students. LAUGHTER.

Hello Prof. Producer and Consumer! Barr-maan! May God bless and preserve you for us. Thanks. And thank you very much indeed . . . Hmm, Nduka, better listen to this whisper: That one going with the empties, he's a real frog. As the frog drinks as much as it croaks, so does he drink as much as he serves. LAUGHTER. Often, he adds his own consumption to the bills of the drunkenly unwary customer or swiftly removes unfinished bottles. Smart fox! That explains his endless praises for your pathological obsession with not having any empty or near-empty bottles on your table while drinking. How that boundless desire for replacement (of 'lost' wines) and sustenance of the euphoria lead to all sorts of suicidal divine inspiration…

Well, I'll obey you and ask our griots about that later.

Now back to our tale! Ehmmm … where were we? You wouldn't remember, coconut head! Oho, it's in the spirit of our age of technological wizardry, which has left us with the memory of pigs, only to rely on papers in libraries, microfilms and other recording devices and computers to process and store information for us … Atrophy here's your trophy: for, unlike your forefathers, you cannot remember important dates without the aid of …

Of course I'm included. Does not one finger which encounters oil soil the rest? But even then, the memory of storytellers is not only commendable—how they are able to keep long tales under control despite digressions and distractions and wines—it is also enriched by the capacity for improvisation where necessary… Why won't you ask me, "what's the use"? Well, I'll here commend the words of my black sister Alice Walker to you: "Storytelling … has a real function. The process

Ah, my friend, my tale still holds on to Akaaga and Sandra in Suite 1013 of Ariya Hotel on a
Sunday morning in July. And Sandra was losing her
patience having to wait for ages to receive payment
for her services.

"Wia my money?" she asked Akaaga son of
Uzi in a voice suffused with Igbo accent. She had
turned away from the world that had engaged her
as she stood by the third-floor window of the hotel. She had steered her thoughts away from toying
with the idea of a *jara*. She now stood before the
dressing table opposite the bed tending the locks of
her wreathed hair before the mirror mounted just
above the table. In the mirror, she could see Akaaga as she made her legitimate demand. But Akaaga
was dozing already.

After toying for a while with her hair, she considered reinvigorating her entertainer-body by

bathing it in the marble bath in the Suite. No! She would rather do the freshening in her own apartment. She had to leave soonest, for she hated being out on Sunday mornings: that time when church-goers busied themselves seeking salvation at various temples or altars. She hated Sunday mornings because it always flooded her mind with guilt and her memory with a bitter remembrance of that Sunday morning one busybody of a man—as she had put it while narrating her experience to her friend with the trade name Tina—insulted her. The man had claimed divine information intimating that she, Sandra, was living a bad life. And that although she might not know it, as other unholy men may never know it too, she exuded a smell akin to the smell of a combination of a billy goat and a dog. She had lived with those searing words ever since. Even when she had tried to dismiss them as the vision of a sinful, false prophet, Sunday mornings confronted her with the words, especially if she was in the streets. In fact, she had developed a sort of phobia for the streets on Sundays. Those unkind words followed her about like the very smell heaped on the fabled billy goat which followed the smart fowl to an ill-fated feast in the land of the blind.

Thus, she urgently needed to collect her money and zoom off to her apartment before the false prophets began their pilgrimage to the churches.

"Which kind *419** nonsense you dey mutter so?" quipped Sandra. Our man was rolling on the hotel bed like an insect being entangled by an adult spider. He was dreaming:

He saw himself seeking the Kingdom of God along a straight, smooth, wide and short road, even when he had been warned by Evangelist Okosun to keep off that road and to take instead the narrow and crooked one which he had neglected at the 'Y' junction. In his characteristic stubbornness, he had taken the one he preferred.

On getting near a gate, he saw a dead tortoise which, save its shell, was already decomposing. He stopped, turned back and saw an orange tree which he had passed in his hurry. He couldn't resist the temptation of going to pluck some of the beautiful- ly ripe and big oranges which were already making him salivate like a dog sighting meat. From under- neath the orange tree he looked up at the luxuri- antly green and thick boughs overhead. He saw two miscreants in school uniform trying to consolidate their positions on strategic branches of the tree.

Before he could ask them what they were doing up there they began to shake the branches of the tree vigorously. And Akaaga son of Uzi got a surprise.

No, no, no, no, nooo, barman. You can't be asking for your cowries now . . . Of course, we know your policy of payments before service. But as 'customership' is concerned, you know. . .? Sure, as my friend has told you, we're not running away . . . And, what's wrong with the bottles. Is it your business also how long it takes us to finish a bottle?

Your 'callers' have no more spaces to sit and their throats are parched, and so what? Well, we're into a spell-binding yarn. Hence, we've forgotten the liquor like the crocodile enamoured with the caresses of the sun forgets water. LAUGHTER.

Okay, my dear Can Themba is already fishing out the cowries from his pockets . . . What's your business with how many names he has? Well, since you care to know, he has as many names as he has favourite authors. Nkosi, how long will it take you to unpocket those cowries? Lord, this redundant habit of keeping cowries in several pockets! Please give the shells to the barman. My tale is yelling for continuation—just like those drunks at the other end of the bar are yelling for more bottles. Yes, settle that bill and leave the rest of the rounds to me . . . Oh, thanks. And, barman, now that the slate's been wiped, could we begin to write on it again? Oh, fine. And do remember while you're supplying the orders that as Nkosi told you a moment ago, even a drunken man has a democratic right to his bottle, at least for all practical purposes.

Besides, he also has the legitimate right to a peaceful and uninterrupted binge no matter how slowly he elects to go about the business . . . God bless you, Dean. You might as well find time to listen to the epic of one of your students who has adopted the spider system of yarn weaving . . . Ehn-ehn! Let me be an Original Perambulator, my friend. But dare you call Nweke Momah that and see what laudable satire the griot will be kind enough to spare you, pretentious voyeur. . .

Didn't I say it before? How temperamental poets can be! Now you're getting angry and impatient again. For, there, the wrinkles come a-rippling again, undulating on your forehead like waves. And, there, your eyes begin to dilate endlessly again, like the swallow's. Haba, Endee! Something is wrong with getting angry and impatient in the theatre . . . Yea, this bar is our theatre and we're both actors and caricatures of sorts, whether you think there's nothing wrong with your reaction or not. And it is the understanding of these facts, including the paucity of good drinkers as there is of good actors and the apparent falsity of our sketches, that links us fraternally happy together as a family . . .

Yea, there you got it. The world is also like a bar. But we'll examine that comparison some other time. Let's get back to our tale. But look! The spool is running out. Better turn it to the flip side before I continue . . . All right if it has an auto-reverse device . . . Good, the flip side is already rolling!

My friend, our man Akaaga son of Uzi, son of Anyibuofu, whose great pestle has pounded many a mortar, received one of the greatest shocks of his life. That's what I'm telling you! The parrot does not forget its notes. Surely not when it repeats them all the time. Repetition is an essential part of my art.

Aha! As those tom-boyish girls shook the tree with all the vigour they could muster, Akaaga's whole body was not only pelted by the oranges which detonated like letter bombs as they landed on him, it was also shrouded by a cloud of *iddos** same way as insects shroud lampposts at night. Akaaga son of Uzi, son of Anyibuofu, began to speak in tongues only spirits could decode. Akaaga began to implore the mercy of his captors. Then Sandra's harsh words ripped the nightmare off his subconscious, and he woke with a start. Poor fellow, he didn't know that the arrow of surprise hides in an ambush.

"What's it?" he asked with the expectancy of a child caught in some mischievous act.

"Nothing but the money! I no fit wait any longer!" Sandra said, struggling into her provocatively slim-fitting mini skirt. Yes, the type that must have inspired the poets, Dele and Walijay, to compose the lines:

Mini, mini, mini skirt,
How I wonder so and fret,
Up above the knees so high,
What's the message for the eye?

Ha! Ha! Ha! Ha!

Akaaga rubbed his eyes with the impulse of a man trying to wipe out a nightmare from his sleepy eyes. He made to get up from the bed then stopped, as if some potent force was insisting on keeping him down in a pinfall until the third, deciding count.

"Listen," he pleaded, drawing Sandra's attention to the frenzied chant of an anguished voice filtering out of the next suite:

*The caged bird knows how sour
the music of captivity tastes in the mouth.
The caged lion knows how futile
prancing about for freedom can be but never gives up.
The buttocks that sits firmly on the ground
knows how empty the threat of the agbisi* is.*

*I am the nut of kola
I am the sand-like nzu*
I am the blood of sacrifice...*

*You're asking, "What could those expressions mean?
What could they portend?" Ah, hold your breath! The
young antelope is breaking its limbs at the rehearsals,
what will it do at the main dance? We shall soon find
out. But, except in a mirror, how do the eyes see the
cars? How? It couldn't have been possible chachalacha!**

Ah, our Queen of Hotels knew better: "Ehen,
Aky, wetin concern me concern wetin dey happen
for hotel room wey no be the one wey I dey?" she
queried. "See wetin time dey talk for your wristwatch. No! Next second no go meet me here o. I
get to commot here now, now-o."

*Does the crow of the cock not warn the sun to begin
its diurnal pilgrimage? MURMURS.*

Our taciturn friend abstractedly reached out for his briefcase. Something in the voice behind the wall however kept prodding his consciousness to unravel. . .

"That's your money," he said, tossing some notes carefreely. His mind was already somersaulting in flashes. Could he have been hearing the voice of a shadow remonstrating with . . . he couldn't puzzle out what or whom. No! It had to be the voice of his wife's *other* in this world. For, he had been made to believe somehow and sometime ago that every living creature is one of a set of twins or triplet. And that, whether the person knew his or her partner(s) or not.

Oh, Nduka, how ingenious the mind is at conjuring atoms of infinite possibilities at fragile moments!

Suddenly, as if in an attempt to satisfy our man's ears, the voice poured forth:

O spirits of our ancestors, come forth
O spirits of our departed dibias, come forth*
with your roots
O spirits of our renowned dibias, come forth
with your herbs
Spill me into your pots

Mix me into your cauldrons
Turn me into your servant
Than let me remain under the spell. . .

Akaaga inched his way to the wall which demarcated his room from the other. He couldn't have cared less whether Sandra picked up the notes or not, whether she left the room or not. Only the power of the voice mattered; only those solemn, incantatory words mattered; only the desire to hear more of it as clearly as possible mattered. He glued his left ear to the wall. And, the invocations tumbled forth. . .

Obida, who dares your potency?*
Ngene, who dares your potency?*
Atachi, who says you're asleep?*
Are you all not the antidote to evil spells?

Oh yeah, keep on hailing me ANTIQUITY. It's well-deserved. After all, is it easy? Were you not chasing the glamour of the city while I spent our school holidays attending village meetings and the singer of tales' performances? Does the child that carries his grandpa's goatskin not quickly learn the wisdom of the elders?

Here you are, a Youth Corps member-cum-journalist, a fully-grown adult not acquainted with the language and culture of his people. Aren't you ashamed?

Akaaga could have been distracted by Sandra's noisy opening and slamming of the door. But he wasn't. The insistent voice on the other side of the wall was still engaging his attention and keeping it afloat as a thread engages a kite and keeps it in the sky:

Come, rain doctors, and keep this evil rain at bay
Come, Mother Earth, and protect me in your womb
Come, you gods, and release me from his spell . . .

Of course, she trusted the potency of faithfully chanted invocations. Had one of her college-days friend's father, a *dibia* from Obamkpa, not informed her that one *dibia* concocts his mixtures, and another neutralises them? She was going to find her man in whichever room he had entered. She was certainly going to prove to him that she was no incarnation of an evil spirit, that he was only temporarily impotent, that he could have an erection for her! *After all, didn't a friend of hers once say that not even God can protect man from erection? LAUGHTER.*

Ah! My friend, in Suite 1013, an uneasy Akaaga dragged himself away from the wall, his head strangely throbbing to the mournful, pathetic rhythm of distant echoes and the inaudible words of the woman. These, fortunately for him, soon faded into the relieving, creaking sound of his neighbour's opening door. He shuffled himself to the window. Slowly, he parted the curtains as Sandra had done moments before and began to look. The thundering and lightning had disappeared the same way they had appeared. But the rain had kept its rhythmic drizzle. On the horizon, the sun was insisting on its legitimate pilgrimage despite the rain. Its progress seemed slow: it was still at an angle in the sky which the eyes could see without the need to slant the head backwards. The streets were deserted: only a few pedestrians and cars could be counted. Christians had assembled in their churches, singing Hosanna to the Lord of Hosts. And Akaaga stood by a window in Ariya Hotel, watching the world.

A rough knock on the door caught his imagination in flight. The knock had a timbre of hostility to it. "What in hell could Sandra want again?" Akaaga asked himself as he walked lethargically towards the door. "Have I not settled her dues? Shall I never have peace of mind in my life? Am I not entitled to some sober reflections on the digressions, the turns my life is. . .?"

Must you vocalise the orders, Nduka? Couldn't you just motion to the barman wem like this . . . to indicate you want a replenishment of the wines? You never would have made a good mute. . .*

Nonsense! Even the billy goat gesticulates and bleats his requests to the nanny goat. And to think of you, a rational being, not being able to communicate effectively . . . I'm not prepared for njakili right now. I know it's one of your hobbies. But let's leave it till after our tale. . .*

Ah, my friend, an eclipse was on the brink! There was confusion between the teacup and the mouth. What! Men in tatters had become nervous at the mere mention of 'madness.' They had begun to perspire in their armpits. . .

Ah, let it break! What do you know about the technology of musical accompaniments in storytelling? My friend, sit down and listen to the modern griot. Our tale has reached a precipice . . . Ah! The kettle was set to call the pot black . . .

Of course, you wished it. Just a moment ago. BUSYBODY. What business of yours is my breaking *the bottle? And so what if the music I produced wasn't blending properly with the . . . ehm . . . What did you call it again. . .? Ehm . . . 'rhythm of expressions?' Who made you a critic of my oral performance? Okay, here our yam-headed barman comes . . . Yea, I'll pay for the bottle. Shikena!* I thank God it isn't the key to my room that broke . . . I'll pay for the bottle. Include it in my bill . . . Ah, listen, sparrow with deaf ears!*

Akaaga flung the door open with the fury of a hurt warlord. Yes! An eclipse was on the brink! Nkemdilim, daughter of Amaechi Nkeonye of Azungwu, stood at the door like a newly bereaved widow. Akaaga's own wife stood before him in a hotel room! His own recently-married wife stood before him in Ariya Hotel, her weary eyes wedged with bags of sleeplessness. *Aha! Now you've known what I've been hoarding.* Our man could well have thought she was an apparition. But no. That voice had warned him. Of course, he had mastered Nkem's voice within the seven months or thereabout that he had contracted the already sour marriage. The voice had never been like that: never been that desperate, never that haunting. And her appearance! He had never seen her wear such a long face, grim like that of a local policeman who hadn't collected

enough toll or tax or bribe—call it what you like—
at a checkpoint by evening, and yet had to *settle** his
*oga** that same evening. *What*! An eclipse was on
the brink! Akaaga's face wore the menacing mask of
a disappointed suitor.

Seconds lapsed with millions of unspoken accu-
sations.

Nkem flashed her beautiful 'torch lights' from a
stupefied Akaaga to her right side of the corridor
and to her left. She could well have been looking
for divine intervention. Or she could well have been
searching for *her man* who had left her out of
frustration to see a friend of his who had checked
into the hotel at the same time as they had the night
before. Whatever it was she was looking for, she was
distracted for a while by the stunningly beautiful
shape of a woman as she disappeared at the end of
the lobby. Ah, she knew! Suddenly, Akaaga's tongue
loosened like a viper's.

"Nkem, what on earth are you looking for here
of all places?"

"*My man!*"

"Shut up!" Akaaga thundered, his eyes springing
hatred.

"I have the right not to answer questions," Nkem

retorted, her electric eyes probing the lobby further.

"Don't you think it is outrightly out of order for you to be here? Who. . .? What on earth were you chanting those invocations for, you itching pants?" Akaaga hissed.

"And you, too, shameless patron of whores. You Playboy of the Third World!" She also hissed. "What is it you have the *exclusive* prerogative to enjoy that I don't have?"

How could she keep quiet? She had opted for the worst. She could no longer withstand the double-standard game of men. She had sworn to return unfaithfulness for unfaithfulness, imprecations for imprecations, love for love . . . That was what compatibility in marriage meant to her. That was what equality of the sexes meant to her! And why should she submit to matrimonial cheating? No, never! Even at the altar during their wedding, she had ogled men as Akaaga had ogled women.

The warning was clear, as clear as teardrops. But Akaaga had thought he would tame her, even if it meant relying on the potency of traditional medicine. That, and the charm which Nkem exuded which had converted him from his no-marriage-for-me philosophy, had encouraged him to sign on the dotted lines. Before Nkem, who although rather plain had the charisma of a godly enchantress, Akaaga had seen women as fruits of pleasure which men had to savour and discard. AIDS or no. He had seen marriage in the light of one journalist's assertion: a pair of stretch jeans easier to get into than to get out of. Not that all that had totally changed for him. But Nkem, the likeable Client Services Manager of Corals, the jet-set advertising agency of the moment, had been exempted and he had gone on to formalise their relationship. Now he knew that the southpaw does not learn to use the right hand in old age. *Mbanu!** One shot of the gun does not kill the warthog quickly enough.

Aha, man! Our friend had married his equal. And the eclipse was on the brink. A bullet had hit the dumb! The unprecedented boldness in his wife's unblinking eyes transfixed Akaaga. Nkem had not exuded such boldness before.

But my friend, the glint in her eyes could shame that mischievous glint of alcohol that flashes forth in your eyes when you laugh under the spell of Saint Bottle . . .

Oh no, the tale has stolen our poet's anger. Now the epic of Akaaga and Nkem in the notorious lobby of Ariya Hotel mocks the epic of Odysseus and Helen on the windy plains of ancient Troy! LAUGHTER.

My friend, that is CHANGE . . . Lord! How the times have changed . . . Oh, it's the people . . . Well, is it not in a machine we're now recording our tale for which your request and the delicious Muse have given me utterance? Besides, spectators can now write while celebrated storytellers are performing. Lord! How much the times have changed! Let me see what you have just scribbled on that torn packet of Trend . . . O Muse, thou art so wonderful: how you give utterance to our poets! Should I read the verse aloud, our soul tortured poets?

In this loom of existence
We weave mats of surprises
Designed with fibres of hope
In tributaries of images.

My goodness! Etching esoteric whispers even on a torn packet of cigarettes? O bacchants! Listen to the words of the Masters of our art, the words of the Masters of our times . . . And those making a noise over there…

Remember, even the ant has a legitimate right to its rantings. Ask Chuba, the Senator. Oh, how the perfume from her dress makes us to digress! Are you listening, Eliot? Aha! I remember doubting Thomas. Our art is not meant for him. He refused to believe that Judas stole the spices for the last supper. If you see him, tell him, please, my dear poet, tell him also that we're still searching for those spices. For the sweeter our supper is, the more our hungry brothers will eat. Thomas must believe that. Repeat it: must believe that!

Ah! The boldness of warlords sends cowards into panic. And Nkem, daughter of Nkeonye the brave one, knew it. Her well-wrought frame of burnished brass knew it and was spoiling for a confrontation, for she had had enough.

"Akaaga the Whore-lord! The snake we killed, into how many bits did we cut it?" she asked.

The floor quaked. Claps of thunder seemed to answer the question for Akaaga. He withdrew into the room and sat on the bed, his weary body ablaze with anger, hatred and disillusionment. His wife had challenged him in the marketplace while the sky was shedding tears.

"Mr. Uzi, what have I done to deserve your attempts at enslaving me since we married, while you prove to be the Whore-lord of Iduu hotels, and society's Minister of Enjoyment? By the way, did *my man* enter this room? I mean, did you by accident see any handsome man with athletic features, plus a hard, shapely bottom pass by?"

Yes, yes, y-e-sss! Nduka, you said it once: when men hurt women it hardly explodes, but when women hurt men's macho egos, the gates of hell are flung open . . .

Akaaga couldn't withstand it. A venial sin is enough to send one to Purgatory. A mortal one condemns him to Hell. Ask Catholics. Within this fractured moment that I'm talking, Akaaga pooled all his strength to advance and launch a thunderbolt-of-a-slap on Nkem's left cheek. The floor quaked! The sound of the slap metamorphosed into raucous reverberations which roused Ariya Hotel to life, as a bugle rouses camping National Youth Service Corps members to life in the mornings. And Nkem bounced to life as if scales had been miraculously cast off her eyes. . .

Asked the poet: "But for how long can the hen wait who's lay is forage for galloping wolves?"

Ah! She pounced on Akaaga, sinking her fangs and claws—weapons that she polished daily—into his face and stomach respectively. Blood seeped out of his flesh jubilantly. O blood, thou art so bloody! The man wearily swung his almost lifeless hands in the air like someone blindfolded. All that remained of his energy after a long, busy night seemed to have been blotted out by that overwhelming pounce from a lioness whose night *partner* had been mysteriously rendered impotent. Had the wise ones not said that hell hath no fury like a woman scorned? Akaaga struggled like this: like a suicide weakened by the noose around his neck. And Nkem tore at him with the fury of a wife who had been driven like a revolting slave.

My friend, the notion of mind-your-own-business preached by the Afrobeat Crown Prince and the soft rhythm of the rain on the rooftop could well have dampened the reaction of the residents of Ariya Hotel to the storm in Suite 1013. But it didn't. No. Not after the spate of violent robberies which had been neglected in the past for similar mind-your-own-business reasons. And, so, many members of staff of Ariya Hotel and some enthusiastic lodgers stormed the war theatre in Suite 1013. They did not want the goat to eat the palm fronds on their heads *yakata** like that. Neither did they want to be told by someone else of the beautiful songs sung at the marketplace...

Yes, that's my praise name: "Antiquity."

And, so, nearly everyone in Ariya Hotel emptied

into Suite 1013 in a legendary show of communal interest. But the eclipse of the sun had taken place in the twinkling of an eye! Akaaga lay on the bed, his limbs stretching to the floor like those of the prey rescued from the leopard by Shaka the Zulu. His strength had been annexed from him.

"It is over! The bondage is over! The court will free me!" Nkem was flashing her 'torch lights' over the male-dominated crowd as she responded to their enquiries. She was looking for her *man*. She did not in the least care about what members of the crowd said. Some were apathetic, some sympathised with Akaaga, while a few others paid compliments to Nkem's courage.

A scream of joy shook the Hotel as Nkem rushed excitedly to embrace her 'handsome man' who had just sidled up to the door of Suite 1013.

"What a disgrace!" "What a mess!" "What a lesson!" The people's reactions to Nkem's behaviour accorded with their *moral* persuasions. And Nkem merged in a blissful embrace with the underwhelmed but unresisting recipient and lodger of Suite 1014 as some of the hotel attendants began to lift Akaaga off the bed. As they brushed past the happy new 'couple', carrying Akaaga away for medical attention, he managed to steal a glance at his *lawful* wife in another man's arms. Then he remembered her strangely consoling words: "It is over! The bondage is over! The court will free me!" But he also remembered something else. "N-nkem," he mumbled, "you should also have . . . known. . ."

But Nkem was too absorbed to be bothered by the *mystery* that 'His Whore-ship' had to reveal.

"You . . . you . . . should also have been aware . . . that . . . that . . . no wo-man, no . . . wo-man ever . . . eats the . . . *Iwu meal** and . . . leaves her . . . hus-band . . . without losing . . . her nose. Nor was any man . . . ever . . . ever able . . . to achieve enough . . . erection to . . . to have her."

Just then, in his mind, a vision of the proceedings of the inevitable customary court drama arose; the possible headlines that papers like *Lagos Weekend* and *Lagos Life* would flash the story with; the gossip that would occupy the public and his friends and colleagues, especially at the office of Edotez Construction Company; all of these and more flowed through arteries of images into the heart of complex probabilities of his 'resurrection' afterwards and the shame that would welcome him.

That is where our tale ends. And barman, you may now play that our favourite Milli Jackson's track, "Fools Affair," while our poet switches off the cassette recorder.

Escapade

*By night on my bed I sought him
whom my soul loveth: I sought him,
but found him not . . .*

— Song of Solomon

SHE paced up and down the large room, her footsteps muffled by the thick rug. She did not care about the presence of other guests. Everything outside her ambition was now insignificant. She chuckled to herself as she eyed the savoury trays of assorted food arrayed on the tables, their colours richer than a rainbow's. She examined her tall frame in the mirror on the eastern wall of the room and was impressed by her appearance. She effervesced with satisfaction; she was cocksure that she had a pronounced wealthy slant. Yes, her ambition was gradually becoming realised. She hated poverty and was determined to fight it with all her might. She disliked lowly and shabbily dressed guys and had always frustrated their overtures. For her, Mr. Right was synonymous with the Prince Charming on modelling magazines. He must be tall, always wear expensive designer clothes, adorn glittering jewels on his wrist, neck, and fingers. He must have a posh sports car. He must. . .

She stole another glance at the mirror. Perhaps she would always admire herself before the mirror each time she passed it. Her shiny silk dress embroidered with tiny golden rings dazzled her eyes. She felt she was really 'arriving.' Then, her thoughts shifted to what could be keeping her sweetheart so long from the party.

Andy had gone to drop Vivian off at her friend's house in his metallic *Baby Benz*. What was happening to him? She kept wondering, trying to believe that Andy could not flirt with Vivian's friend. She had heard that she was a seductress! Distrust began to sink its taproot into her. She tried to dismiss such thoughts. But they persisted. She was determined not to let any ugly thoughts mar the night. After all, she had dreamt so much about the dinner party . . . how she would sample every bit of food; how she would prove to Andy that she was more sophisticated and more exposed than any of the girls he had gone out with—in many other ways than just smoking; how she would outshine the other girls at the party; how she would make them jealous. . .

"It's good to see you, Tina," one of her old school-mates interrupted her wandering thoughts.

"Ah! Pat, is it you? I thought you'd not make it, that you'd be too busy at the hospital."

"Well, when you rang and said you'd be here to-day with Andy, I took the day off that was due to me. I felt it would be an opportunity and a pleasure to meet your much-talked-about Andy. Where is he?"

"Oh! He's gone to drop Vivian off at her friend's place. You remember Vivian Ekene, that garrulous and ever-jealous friend of mine at St. Louis? He'll soon be back."

"Wow! You are looking like a model. Really smashing," Patricia was captivated by Tina's appearance and, to her own surprise, had expressed it in a voice devoid of envy.

"Thanks for the compliment, my dear Pat. This red dress, this pair of shoes and this handbag to match were among the last batch of gifts Andy brought me from Paris."

"You are lucky to have him. He must be a nice

guy. Perhaps you'll marry him."

"Let's go and sit down in that corner," Tina suggested, avoiding discussing the new topic and trying to suppress the tension that was mounting inside her. For all she knew, she was not prepared to settle down, at least not while she was still in school. She thought of herself as an adventuress who still had to explore spinsterhood. Perhaps she would change her mind later. But certainly not now.

They sat down in a corner from where they could see whoever entered the room. They talked about the life they had led and their futures, punctuating their discourse with gossip about each guest that entered the room.

"That girl who entered now with that man in a grey suit wanted to snatch my Andy."

"You don't mean it! And what happened?"

"What do you expect? Andy just had fun with her and discarded her like a used pad. You don't expect him to go out with that wretch, do you?"

Just then, Andy entered the room with a charming girl whose waist he had almost encircled with his right hand. He had forgotten himself, for the girl could steal a lecherous man's heart. She was remarkably beautiful, and her contagious smile emphasised her beauty. Her eyes were blazing softly like a late October afternoon sun. Her cheeks were decorated with light shades of make-up. Her oval face crowned an astonishing hourglass shape and harmonised with her beautiful and carefully carved curves. The nipples of her full breasts seemed to be interrogating her simply designed *adire* outfit. Her skin was dark brown and smooth to some extent: a few pimples and blackheads dotted her face. Her dentures shone like polished brass and her smile, although a little awkward, seemed laced with confidence.

"Tina, meet Funke, Vivian's friend. She is a banker," said Andy, smiling mischievously.

"Hello!" Tina said, managing to suppress her nervousness.

"Hello!" Funke replied.

"So, who is your friend, Tina?"

"She's Pat. Patricia Ivbiye, a schoolmate at St. Louis. She is a nurse at *U.C.H.** Pat, meet my Andy."

Andy exchanged greetings with Pat, trying to stifle an expression of disapproval of Tina's possessiveness. He quickly brooded over how best to handle the sticky situation. For, while he was dropping her off, Vivian had encouraged him to allow her friend Funke join him to the party 'to distract her from the heartbreak she had recently suffered.' And he had reluctantly accepted. As they were driving to the venue of the party at New Bodija, he had contemplated jilting Tina. He had justified such a decision through his own peculiar logic: she was too materialistic; he had swallowed enough embarrassment brought by rumours of her flirtations; she would be an obstacle to his new plan. Yes, he ought to abandon Tina. He had to drop the bomb! But how? He would provoke her temper, then as a reaction to it, shock her with his decision.

He preferred Funke, no doubt. If his technique of mind-reading was anything to rely on, she had some homegirl qualities—collected, meek, and respectable. Perhaps, innocent. Besides, she had a soul. He ogled her and grinned as they served themselves at table. "Sure, she's a super lady," he mumbled to himself. "Sure, the bomb has to come."

THE dark room seemed chilly and hostile. She woke with a start. But why would she wake so soon when she ought to be in the depths of sleep as a

result of the night's hassles? she asked herself sadly. The silence in the room told her that her roommates were yet to return from the party they had
gone to at Ring Road. Not wanting to think about
the good time they would be having at the party, she
shut her eyes and prayed for sleep to assail her and
carry her to oblivion. But sleep would not come.

She stared into the dark, pondering the night's
sour dinner party. Did she really merit that dressing
down by Andy? Why did it have to happen before
Pat? Did she succeed in upsetting Andy by flirting with Chief Adetunji? But she only wanted to
avenge the mental agony Andy had subjected her to
by ignoring her and, thus, make him jealous. Why
did she make such a mistake? Perhaps if she had
contained Andy's excesses, he would not have burst
out at her the way he did. No, she should not have
lost control of herself. But she had not been able to
bear the sight. She had wanted to prove her worth.
What had Andy said? "You shameless, sex-selling
whore who doesn't know the ideals of modesty,
you think you're fooling me?" Only that fragment
echoed in her mind. His voice had reverberated. In
her surprised state, she had not been able to utter
a word. Ordinarily, she would have railed. But she

was stunned; she had been caught unawares. She had wept. Did Funke and Pat see those tears that marred her make-up? Did Chief Adetunji know what had happened?

She rose from her bed, went to the window and pulled the thick curtains apart. Rays of light filtered into the room, falling upon a portrait of Andy that hung just above her pillows. She took the portrait and destroyed it. She did not want to be reminded of Andy by that *piece of paper*. She had to close that chapter of her life now. After all she was Y.S.F. (Young, Single and Free). Besides, she was sufficiently good-looking. "Did I say good-looking?" she soliloquised, her mind flashing back to Funke's beauty. It saddened her all the more.

She returned to her bed to try to get some more sleep. But her thoughts disturbed her. She compared Andy with Chief Adetunji and sadly admitted that Andy was better. He was younger and in a better position to shower her with gifts because he travelled widely as an importer of goods manufactured overseas, especially in China. But did she know much about the Chief? Chances were that he could also maintain her. And, if he didn't live up to expectations? Well, she had resolved never to live below her current standard. She was determined to rise above her social class, so what did it matter how she went about it? At two in the afternoon, she would go to visit Chief Adetunji. It would cost her a hundred naira each way by a special taxi drop, and she would be very tired after experiencing traffic jams in the blazing sun. But the journey would be worth it. Besides, her tiredness after that would help her sleep soundly at night.

Chief Adetunji had offered to take her to Premier Hotel and she had accepted the offer. As the car—a glittering, big, black BMW—climbed the hill which led to the hotel from the Cultural Centre end, she concluded in her mind that alcohol would help her get over her emotional stress, shore up her courage and impress the Chief with the idea of her maturity and level of exposure. She would make a request for any kind of rum, preferably Jamaican. If it was not in stock, she would make do with gin and lime or any rich cocktail.

"What's your favourite dish, Tina?" Chief asked as they sat on a reddish sofa.

"I am afraid, Tunji, I don't have a favourite dish. I am equally attracted to all delicacies," she said in a very mellow tone, looking up to see Chief's reaction. She added, "But I think I always enjoy chicken 'n' chips. What about you?"

Chief Adetunji explained that he was dieting because of his big size, which nevertheless seemed to blend with his protruding belly. Were he a member of the Pregnant Men Association of Nigeria as constituted by a cartoonist, he would have belonged to the Baba Ibeji group.

They placed the orders for food and drinks, which the waiter brought without wasting time. Tina gulped tots of gin and lime over a plate of *chicken peri-peri.** Chief sipped from a glass of club soda.

"How do you like the combination, T?"

"It's fine," she purred. "I am enjoying every bit of it. The soup is quite richly spiced, and the gin is original. You know, most Gordon's Gin these days are adulterated."

They chatted on about nothing.

After some time, Tina's eyes began to droop. Chief Adetunji noticed them and felt his passion rising. The revolver between his thighs began to revolt, kicking and panting. He put down the glass of soda and slipped his hands into his pockets. He discreetly tried to control his revolting trigger. Then he suggested that they go upstairs.

As they sauntered into a luxuriously furnished suite, Chief Adetunji grew hot with desire. Inside the room, he fondled an unresisting Tina who swooned with erotic abandon. Soon, they capsized into the oblivious abyss of physical passion.

IT was madness to turn to drink and sugar daddies as props. She should have known that they would ultimately make her depressed—if not hysterical— and unable to cope with the boiling cauldron of conflict between her and Andy. What she had begun as a temporary escape was becoming a habit. She discovered to her amazement that she could now consume pints upon pints of alcohol before becoming intoxicated. And she used any excuse to empty glasses of spirits.

One dull Sunday evening, she had a row with Bunmi, her dearest roommate. Bunmi had decided to talk to her about her lousy lifestyle. Tina did not care for any of it. Rather, in her characteristic rage, she spurted abuse at the concerned girl. To assuage her anger, she decided to go out and have a drink since she had none in the room. She thought briefly about her destination and settled on seeing Dr. Owoyemi. He was a light-hearted, rich Commissioner who knew how to transport her out of her melancholic moods. He was her so-called 'new flame.'

The thought of having such a highly-placed man gladdened her heart. But that was only momentarily, for the infernal emotional war continued to rage in her as she trotted to the reception lounge.

At the hall's reception she dialled Dr. Owoyemi's number. The Commissioner picked up after the third ring.

"Hello! Good evening," he said in a collected voice.

"Hello, Willy!" she said, recognising his voice. "Good evening! I am feeling very depressed. Would you trip the light fantastic for me?" She recalled an old school slang. "I'll be waiting for—"

"What the hell is wrong with you, Tina?" Dr. Owoyemi thundered. "How many times have I told you not to call my house? Supposing my wife answered the call, who the hell would you tell her you are? After all those rumours she's heard? Listen, Tina, I am through with you. It would be wiser for you to seek your fun elsewhere. And, with a more serious fellow—some guy who is prepared to settle down with you. Enough is enough!"

Tina froze on the spot. Had she heard him correctly or were her ears deceiving her? She held her breath briefly in a frantic effort to confirm that he had not merely paused to ensure that there were no eavesdroppers as he usually did. Yes, she bitterly admitted at last, the line was dead. Dr. Owoyemi had hung up on her.

As she walked wearily back to her room with a downcast face, evil thoughts competed for supremacy in her mind.

TINA'S spirit was uplifted as she drained the last glass of gin and lime in her best friend's room where she had gone to seek solace. Her gloomy disposition began to give way to a desire to avenge the torture of her heart and the collapse of her world, for so she felt. She had been incubating this desire for vengeance for a good long time, but it had never been as strong as it was now. Perhaps today was the best day to hatch it, she thought. Apart from such an act making the day a fateful one indeed, she was in the best mood to confront that so-called Andy. "Sure, he deserves it," she thought. "I'll give it to him."

She boarded a bus to the gate. Hired a taxi there and directed it to Andy's house at Onireke. The thought of the events of the last few hours agitated her and inflamed her anger as the taxi journeyed forth.

She pressed the doorbell and waited for a response. For some reason, Andy opened the door without questioning who his visitor was.

"Good evening, Tina. May I know what you want?" he asked casually, trying to hide his disappointment.

"Yes, Mr. Andrew Osagie," she said, trying hard to suppress her escalating contempt for the name and its bearer. "I want to know what you told Dr. Owoyemi about me. I understand you play tennis with him at the recreation club."

"What are you talking about? Are you crazy?" Tributaries of anger flooded Andrew's mind.

"Look, I have no time to waste on you. Just apologise for all you've done to me or I'll get even."

"Okay, if it's trouble you want, I'll give you a good dose of it." The torrent of anger in his mind rose as he spoke. He made to force Tina out of his house.

Tina clung stubbornly to the doorpost, retorting: "We'll settle our score today. We'll pay our dues." She was sweating and swelling with untold hatred for Andy.

"You and who?" Andy issued a dirty slap to her face.

Tina, in a mad fury, brandished a pen knife attached to her key holder and plunged it into Andy's chest. He stumbled and slumped to the floor. Blood flowed from the open wound, drenching a portion of the wine-coloured rug. She stared at him for a while then impulsively stooped to feel his pulse. As she did so, Andy groaned and passed out. She was terrified, and tears began to stream from her eyes, blurring her vision.

She had collected herself too late. What would she do now? she wondered as her mind became a labyrinth of mind-blasting thoughts: What sort of fiery temper is this? What have I done? What would I be living for? To live and pay for my sins or to plunge into the other world? Yes! That is a better option. What an idiot I have been! I can't live a shameful life. I can't stand the world. I would rather take my life. Perhaps I'll overtake Andy in his slow journey to the Almighty Judge's court.

She rushed into Andy's dining room, picked up a bottle of drugs, and without caring what kind of medication they were, dashed to the refrigerator in the corner of the dining room. She removed a bottle of big stout from the fridge and emptied the drugs in the bottle into her mouth. Then, without bothering about a cup, she gulped them down with the stout. She coughed and swallowed hard. She dashed to the bar and brought out a bottle of hard liquor from a shelf. She unscrewed the cork and poured what remained of it into her mouth. Still not satisfied, she rushed to the kitchen, looked around and found a small bottle of *ota pia pia*.* She unscrewed the cork and downed the rodent poison. "Sure, that will hasten my exit," she concluded.

Somebody knocked on the door at that point and, without waiting for an answer, went in through the door which had been left ajar. On seeing Andy on the floor with his shirt dyed in blood, she screamed.

"What's wrong, Funke?" her companion asked, rushing into the room.

"Andy . . . has be-en ki-ll-ed," she managed to say between sobs. She lay her head on Andy's chest, not minding his blood-soaked shirt. "Call . . . call the police, Vivian."

As Vivian hastened to the telephone set atop a chest of drawers that marked off the sitting-room from the dining, she noticed Tina lying on the floor, her cold eyes staring vacantly.

"Oh, Funke, it's Tina. Must be a case of murder-suicide." There was urgency in her voice as she uttered the words while dialling the police emergency number.

When she was through, she came over to Funke who was writhing on the floor. She tried to console her.

"Oh, Vivian! I've . . . never . . . never seen such a bloody . . . such a bloody sight before," Funke spurted, sobbing and writhing on the blood-stained rug.

Fatal Birth

When the sea murmurs plaintive tones,
Of ecstasy, at the golden sinews of dawn!
Far, by the cornfields, a shadow re-echoes
The dream of the past . . .

— Ntogela D. Masilela

NDIDI Nwachukwu's sanity may actually have become unhinged after the 14th of February when she was delivered of a stillborn baby—a monster at that—instead of the 'bouncing baby boy' that she and her live-in lover, Dapo Ekundayo, had longed and prayed for. They had lived together for about four years and Dapo, a clearing and forwarding agent, had been somewhat patient. Still, he would not wed her until she got pregnant. Those barren years of hers had been very agonising. They had spent much of it visiting various trado-medical doctors and spiritual churches, until Supreme Evangelist Akabuogwu performed the miracle. And they knew joy!

Dapo had immediately ordered her wedding gown from New Era Designers, one of the best fashion designers in the country, to mark the news or what he had described as 'ND's most important and happy revelation.' Thereafter, he'd booked a thanksgiving service at the church. After the service, the Supreme Evangelist informed them of a vision he received during the service. His disclosure had been arresting:

"Sad as it may be, the will of the Lord must be done. You must postpone further arrangements for the impending ceremony till the baby boy arrives. Mr. Ekundayo, you shall in the near future reveal the D-Day, as the Lord of Hosts shall direct you in a dream. There shall be a celebration of the baby's birth with your wedding. Meanwhile, be rest assured that the Lord has spiritually blessed and united you two loving, young hearts. One more thing, though. You shall present to the Lord the following items in thanksgiving and for further prayers. . ."

"But where has all that led us to? A mind-blasting, monstrous stillborn!" Ndidi thought, wincing for the umpteenth time and scratching her long, tousled hair abstractedly. Then she let fly, addressing imaginary figures in the bedroom.

"And what have our few relations in town done? Sporadic visits in the first few days following the incident, and then rumour mongering. 'She's an *ogbanje**... She's an *abiku**... There's a curse hanging on her neck that whoever visits—'

"Even in Lagos?" She spat onto the rug and scratched her itchy hair absentmindedly. She rolled from one edge of the bed to the other. "What an experience! And why me?" she moaned.

The cryptic experience could not have been more hallucinatory for the thirty-four-year-old, tall, dark, plump and pretty schoolteacher. For, since then she had suffered mental replays of the mind-bending horror film clip of their journey in Dapo's new Pathfinder to Oluwa Seun Clinic: He had had that unprecedented gleeful radiance on his face as he anticipated the birth of their pearl of inestimable value, also to be known as Dapo Jr., which kept expanding, filling the jeep; Clip of the reassuring voice of Dr. Segun Owode metamorphosing into convoluted jargon: "Braun's blunt-pointed scissors, the midwifery forceps ... It's been a case of embryotomy, a case of a double-headed monster;" Clip of herself wrapped in sterilised sheaths, while springs of hot tears burnt Dapo's eyes.

"Lord, these details! This most horrible film is unbearable. Relieve me, O Lord," she often prayed.

One beautiful evening, about a fortnight after she returned from the clinic, Ndidi decided at last to do some practical things to release herself from the bondage. First, she tried to exorcise her heart by pouring it out in a detailed letter to Nwaka, her favourite friend of longstanding who had left for London. Then she contemplated suicide as usual but could not muster the courage to go through with it.

She picked up one of the bestseller paperbacks Dapo had bought to help her ward off those recurrent hallucinations she suffered in the lonely times until her maternity leave expired and she was strong enough to get quite busy again.

The story began to reel off before her like a motion picture being fast-forwarded. Hallucinations. She saw herself as a harlequin in the stead of the heroine of the novel. And she was walking on a beach! She threw the fat volume on the sofa and hurried into the living room. Spell-bound by the strange passion to walk on a beach, she opened the wardrobe in the room. The sight of her wedding gown still awaiting that nebulous day when her most secretive master of surprises, Dapo, would take her to the altar infuriated her. She seized the gown and tore it. Then she took out one of her most expensive dresses on impulse and put it on as she shuffled towards the dressing table. Her trembling hands caused one of the copper-plated, razor-blade-shaped earrings to fall under the table when she tried to put it on. She bent down to pick it up and her eyes caught a red book improperly tucked underneath the maroon carpet. It was Dapo's life, his time-worn diary filled with his secrets. Out of an uncharacteristic urge, she opened it and read, and read, and read...

The revelatory entries ripped her already over-burdened mind with anguish, uncorked the tears in her eyes and fuelled her with a burning disgust for life. She tore a blank page from the diary and scribbled her soul onto it before putting the final full stop to her capital resolution: FAREWELL, MY LOVE.

Ndidi dropped the note on the dust-covered table. She took a long reluctant look at the mirror before leaving that posh apartment in Victoria Island Extension, Maroko, which Dapo had moved into following the recent windfall he got from a deal. The area had been brutishly claimed from the less-privileged dregs of the land by Colonel Risky Bulldozer, the former Military Governor of the State. Without her rouge, or any other make-up, Ndidi's face bore a strange, childlike innocence. And her beautiful dress, a classic *mama-dash-me,** suited her as if it were customised for her by a gifted designer. It had never looked so good. She laughed in spite of herself, wondering aloud: "But what does it really matter? Aren't things generally out of joint in this tumbled gamble of a life?"

Meanwhile, Nsikak, the housekeeper, and Sule, the gatekeeper, were out enjoying a fight in the neighbourhood, leaving the gate ajar.

Not reckoning with the seeming signals of metaphysical assistance, Ndidi boarded a *kabu-kabu** that had in no time pulled up before her at the bus stop. As the poorly maintained Peugeot 504 cab groaned along the road to Bar Beach, she stared at the horizon through the window. On the far side, a fading sun sending out its last diurnal rays seemed to be bidding the earth farewell.

As darkness fell, the *kabu-kabu* lumbered to a halt at the bus stop by the Beach. Ndidi hopped out. She crossed the road. Beside a shed at the beach, she pulled off her shoes. Then she looked around the beach once more. There were a couple of silhouettes—and the sea! But then the sea, through some hallucinatory transformation, appeared as a cinema screen before her very eyes. Another clip: The blood-stained, monstrous stillborn of hers holding a burnt breast and wailing for HELP. . .

Mindblast! Unable to bear the sight anymore, she dived in the direction of the mystery child, shouting: "Blood is thicker than water!"

Just then, Dapo rushed to the scene. But all he heard and had were, respectively, the fast-fading echoes of his beloved's voice and the lurid farewell note she had dropped.

Just Above A Drunk

(for 'Professor' Johnson, the
producer and consumer)

Outside here, life is snobbish,
like a five-star hotel.

— Afam Akeh

THEY were in Madam Okiti's *buka*. The shack was located somewhere in the Agbowo area of Ibadan, a shack wedged between two dilapidated houses. They always came there at dusk to drown the sorrows and failures of the day, or to 'wash' the joys and successes of the day. One of them collected yet another bottle of the stale palm wine from the dishevelled Madam Okiti and set it on the low table. He lazily lifted the bottle and poured some of the 'holy water' into a well-carved calabash. He raised the calabash to a perfect angle and guzzled the liquid. He then took a break, as he usually did, to wish it a safe journey down to his bowels. His stomach rumbled as if in acknowledgement. He belched, cleared his throat, then said:

"Let's talk about women."

"Tafioko, you never tire of talking about women," said one of them, wiping the sweat that was oozing out of his head like water from a soaked sponge.

"Okay!" Tafioko downed another calabash of the stale palm wine and belched again before continuing, "Let's talk about our . . . rulers then. No! Let's talk politics."

"Oh, that's better," a pot-bellied man complimented. Beside him was a slightly drunk whore whose skin reflected the corrosive effects of bleaching creams. As the man made to kiss her, she flicked out her tongue like a lizard about to catch a fly and licked the man's tongue dry of spittle.

"Pol-itics! Bobs, I always like talking about . . . politics and . . . women," said Tafioko in a stentorian voice. His eyes dilated like an owl's as he tried to figure out the drunken man who was sleeping beside him in a corner of the *buka*. For, as the man slept, his snores rose and fell rhythmically like the rehearsed tune of a trumpeter.

"Bobs . . . that Bob in that corner is . . . I mean he's . . . how do you say it . . . Dead. Yea, Bobs, he's dead . . . fine."

"Yes, Bobs, he's passed out," said the pot-bellied man, caressing the whore beside him.

"That's all right, Bobs," said the sweating man. Tafioko you were, ehm . . . about talking politics. . ."

"Yes, Bobs, pol-itics. Okay . . . now I'll talk about . . . ehm . . . our rulers. The bosses. They're . . . all THIEVES."

"Thieves?" questioned the whore.

"Yes, THIEVES!" reiterated Tafioko, rising furiously from the dirty bench. He wiped his Hitler-like moustache with the back of his left hand then continued in his well-known outspokenness. "Bobs, I know better now . . . ehm, the people know better now. Last . . . aha! . . . last Friday night, I was passing the MESS . . . Ah-ah! No! It was the Headquarters. Then I managed to catch a glimpse of. . ."

"Good efnign-o," interrupted a client as he entered the *buka*. "Madam Okiti, one botul of strong Barry White with saccharine for me. One botul for Tafioko."

Tafioko burst into laughter. He measured his steps as he walked to the opposite end of the *buka* where his short, dark benefactor was now seated and shook his hand appreciatively. He then waddled back to his position, lifted up the brown bottle with a slightly trembling hand and poured some more drink into his calabash. He raised the calabash up strenuously and sent the white liquid into his stomach with urgency.

"Bobs, *aki* is go-o-d," Tafioko commended the palm wine, altering the rhythm of his voice like a syncopated jazz rhythm.

"Ta-fioko the consumer. Lover of aki for alcohol," hailed the man.

"Kolo, you've come to divert Tafioko from the interesting story he was telling us," said another man who had scarcely uttered a word. "You're always fond of doing this," he added, recoiling like a python about to pounce.

"Sorry o," apologised Kolo as he settled down to his drink.

"Ehen, Tafioko, you were . . . ehen . . . talking about the . . . bosses," reminded the sweating man.

"Where did I . . . stop?" asked Tafioko.

"Oho! You managed to see . . ." prompted the whore.

"Ehen . . . I managed . . . a glimpse of . . . ehm . . . a glimpse of the inside."

Madam Okiti rested a full bottle of the stale

palm wine Kolo had ordered for Tafioko before him. He giggled, eyed Kolo gratefully, then continued more heartily. "Bobs, what I saw was . . ." he battled for the right word.

"What did you see?" asked the sweating man, impatiently.

"Bobs, steak and chicken were being grilled in a corner. They arrested my attention. So. . ." He swallowed hard, belched, then continued, "so I . . . ehm . . . glued myself to a tree . . . that tree now, and watched them. By then . . . Bobs, wake up and hear this . . . this interesting gist and stop snoring like . . . ehm . . . a prisoner subdued by hard labour." Tafioko shook the man who was sleeping beside him vigorously. The man grunted, raised his head reluctantly and rested it again on the wet table. Others laughed thunderously.

"He's . . . ehm . . . how did you say it? . . . ehm . . . 'passed out,'" said Tafioko, still laughing.

"So, by then. . ."

"Oho! As I was saying . . ." Tafioko poured some drink into his calabash and continued, ". . . ehm . . . my mouth was watering like a dog's when it sees a fat bone." He took a sip from the calabash, coughed, then shook his head sideways as if to clear the haze in it. "I was salivating seriously. You would think I . . . ehm . . . I had some illness. I saw all their big-big cars. Benz. No, not Benz . . . ehm . . . that new one they call . . . ehm . . . ehm . . . *Baby Benz*. No, it has a new name . . . It's the latest model in town. Remember it . . . blockheads."

"Oya, forget the name," somebody quipped.

"Okay, forget the name," another supported.

"No . . . ehm . . . 'The Beast' . . . I saw that one. I saw . . . ehm . . . I saw their plenty expensive . . . and flashy cars all parked inside the . . . Headquarters' compound."

"Don't you think that . . . they bought them with their salaries?" asked the whore, righting some stray strands of her elegantly coiffed, brownish hair.

"Stupid question!" shouted somebody in a loud and harsh voice which rang out across the room like peals of thunder. It was greeted by seconds of untold silence.

"Bobs, that's how . . . the bosses talk to . . . us." Tafioko broke the silence, sending everyone except the whore into laughter.

"Tafioko, go on bo," reminded the sweating man whose jumper was then almost glued to his body.

"Bobs, where did . . . did I stop?"

"You saw their plenty costly cars."

"Bobs, inside the parlour . . . that heavenly furnished parlour, they were . . . ehm . . . partying. Bobs, they were . . . I mean, partying seriously. And somewhere, the steaks and chicken were dripping oil . . . very fresh. You see, Bobs, that's why . . . ehm . . . what do I always say?"

"Heaven and hell are in this world," answered Kolo, then hailed him, "Tafioko!"

"Bobs, thank you." Tafioko gulped up what was left in his calabash and refilled it. "Bobs, there's heaven . . . and . . . there's hell in this country. Bobs, that was . . . heaven. What could I . . . I do but ehm . . . go closer to have a fuller view?"

"I wish you were caught," said the whore casually.

"Your papa!" cursed Tafioko.

Someone entered the *buka* and wished everyone a good evening. They didn't seem to notice him.

"If I . . . I . . . hear any PIM again from you, Phina . . . you'll regret the . . . the day you were born. *Ashawo bas-s-t-a-r-d.*"* When Tafioko had said this, his temper abated. Phina knew better than to reply. Nobody ever dared Tafioko whose body was built like that of Superman of the children's comic fame.

"Nobody should interrupt again . . . until Tafioko

finishes his story," decreed the diminutive, sweating man. "Ehen . . . Tafioko, you were talking about . . . ehm . . . how you went closer to have a fuller view . . ."

"Bobs, I couldn't believe what . . . my eyes saw . . . ehm . . . ehm . . . MONEY . . . *Muri-Muri** Nothing but . . . *Muri-Muri* and *Wazobia.** The bosses were . . . ehm . . ." He rose from the bench and began to wave his hands in the air. "Bobs . . . they were . . . ehm . . . spraying wads on those . . . those fat-breasted . . . and . . . ehm . . . fat-*ikebe** women, plus . . . some small-small girls."

As he was waving his hands, demonstrating as if almost entranced how the bosses were spraying money on women, some of who were of easy virtue, Tafioko lost his balance and fell. He tripped over some bottles in the process. When they helped him up, he staggered. Unable to stagger farther, he slumped onto the bench beside Phina. Excitedly he began to fumble with Phina's breasts.

"Bobs . . . the bosses . . . are . . . ehm . . . ehm . . . ehm . . . THIEVES. Bobs, I'm . . . go-ing to . . . lie on these pil-lows. Bobs, no-no . . . Bobs, a . . . a breast in hand . . . is . . . ehm . . . worth two . . . in . . . ehm . . . the bra. Ask Oga Joe the humorous one."

"Tafioko!" hollered the pot-bellied man, getting

angry. But Tafioko would not free Phina's breast which he had fully cupped with his hands. The pot-bellied man shook him vigorously, taking care not to hurt Phina.

"Please help! He's mad or something," Phina blurted out.

"Bobs," bellowed Tafioko, "this . . . this . . . ehm . . . how the bos-ses . . . ehm . . . rocked them. Bobs . . . the bos-ses . . . ehm . . . ehm . . . yes . . . they . . . steal . . . our . . . money."

It took the combined efforts of two men to liberate Phina from Tafioko's hold and to toss him off. Having lost his motor coordination now, he tottered for a while and fell to the ground, retching.

"Tafioko the CONSUMER!" Kolo mocked.

"Bobs, the . . . bos-ses . . . enjoy . . . my wealth . . . our . . . sweat . . . at ehm . . . the MESS . . . Bobs, while . . . we're frantic to find, ehm . . . a meal to . . . ehm . . . quench . . . our . . . thirst . . . they're fran-tic to ehm . . . re-tain . . . po-wer . . . to . . . sup-ply ehm . . . themselves . . . lux-uries . . . Bobs . . . but . . . do we . . . ehm . . . I mean . . . ehm . . . do we have . . . anyone to . . . to . . . to. . ."

Before he could finish, he drifted into a laboured sleep as the *buka* patrons departed one after the other, leaving him and Madam Okiti.

And she was busy clearing the mess in the *buka*.

Just Before the Desert Storm

*"You can't eat hope," the woman said.
"You can't eat it but it sustains you,"
the colonel replied.*

*— Gabriel Garcia Marquez, No
One Writes to the Colonel*

ONWUKA *Amadi looked out of the window and smiled. In a region of his mind, a story began to unfurl.*

IT was the eve of the Gulf War and nobody seemed to mind the colour of the sky that late evening. Dark, loose wools that they had become, the clouds hurried westward as if shying away from either the fast-fading dusk or from impending rain, or both. And it was the time of the year when, normally, the August break seizes the rains. But not this August. Every roll of the gathering clouds left hints of rain in the horizon, and with it, a gathering fear. BE-WARE, THE IDES OF AUGUST! a newspaper banner had screamed on July 31. And it had been right. It had been a most cruel day, that day that coalition forces had massed up on the Saudi-Iraq border, itching for the 'Mother of all Battles.' Several disasters had struck that day.

Chiedu looked up from where he sat on a dusty bench in a corner of the large hall. Where his friend Oni sat, he could see the strains in his philosophical eyes. As Dambudzo Marechera would say, the acids of gut-rot had eaten into the base metals of his brain, and his blazing eyes were an outward testimony to that fact.

With some effort, Chiedu rose from the bench, stared out through the panes of the high window at the sheet of clouds, then began to sing Okigbo's lines:

Messiah will come again
After the argument in heaven
Messiah will come again. . .

From one of the houses adjoining the multi-pur-pose Izu Hall, a voice blaring from a radio was insistent on drowning Chiedu's, or so it seemed. It was a sad, trembling voice, for all he could make of it. But then a remarkable ring of decisiveness around it reminded him of Major Gideon Orkar's voice as he 'excised' the northern states from Nigeria during the aborted coup of April 22, 1990.

But for the reverberating voice, the occasional shrieks and cackles of street urchins, silence dwelled in the air. Columns of people could be seen standing on their toes in the lobby of the house from where the voice emanated. And, like children awaiting the result of their promotion exams, anxious syllables that held no sound was spelled boldly on their faces.

Chiedu beckoned to Oni as he sauntered out of Izu Hall.

"What's the matter?" His voice quavered as he approached the scene.

Nobody answered.

Wriggling his way into one of the columns, he listened too. Oni had followed him, absentmindedly staring at his rubber wristwatch as he walked. It was a little past seven in the evening. And there was everything in the brooding weather to indicate that the world was on the brink of ruin. By the time Oni got to the gathering, an argument had sprung up.

"What do we do now?" A robust family man seemed to be most worried.

For God-knew-how-many-times within forty-eight hours, the villagers' peace of mind was shattered. Matters had now gone beyond rumours. It was not just about the confirmation of the death of the seven men who sought a way out through suicide when, the day before, the authorities swooped on the vaults of Resources Managers—the extraordinary bankers who had paid their customers' unbelievable interest within a record time—but of the declaration of war on Iraq by the Allied Forces led by America. If rumour was all that it was, the people might have opted for the *siddon-look** stance. But the Voice of America (VOA) broadcast had reported that the Iraqi leader Saddam Hussein was threatening to use nuclear and chemical warheads in what Professor Johnson dubbed 'the mother of all battles,' as he expatiated on the news to the villagers who had trooped to his house. It also revealed that America and Israel had not only equipped their citizenry with gas masks but had threatened to return fire for fire, missile for missile.

As it was, picturing the scenario terrified the villagers in whose memories were still lodged the Hiroshima and Nagasaki holocausts. For them, there seemed to be no escape from the lethal plague which Professor Johnson, in his learned analysis, had predicted would afflict the world. For the Wizard of Book, as some of the villagers fondly hailed him, was reputed to be so dead accurate in his prophecies that he was revered by many and regarded by some as a demi-god—the most outstanding *son of the soil.* Worse still, he had compared the people's fate with that of the 15 shipwrecked men in Theodore Gevicault's *The Raft of the Medusa.* And he proudly illustrated his prophecy with the imitation of the great, disturbing painting which hung in a most visible part of his sitting room.

"Let's hold the end-of-the-world party." The words escaped from the lips of an otherwise taciturn leader of the Elders' Council, Diokpa Pa Okekumatulor. "Our ancestors will not receive our spirits if we perish SCARED of the devious designs of some mad white people. It's an ABOMINATION in this land to die thinking of the mysterious powers of the white man."

"But it is irrational," protested Professor Johnson, a volcano of anxiety welling up inside him. "It will be tantamount to madness to hold such a party just because you know that destruction is in the wind. Hasn't Andre Brink, the South African writer, said it all before? To know is not enough. One must try to understand too."

"What's there to understand?" retorted one of the youths present. "Are the words of the elders no more words of wisdom?" He stressed the last word as much as his coarse voice would let him.

"When life becomes an incurable disease what sense is there in waiting with long faces for the foul thud of white men's weapons of mass destruction?" another elder reasoned.

"But things could change; some truce may be reached," argued Professor Johnson.

"Away with book knowledge!" Chief Asielue thundered. "In the beginning, superior knowledge belonged to our ancestors, until white people stole up on us with their congealed memory and culture deposited in sepulchral books. How shall it be told that we perished AFRAID of death by some mad invention of some lunatics? Shall we be brave enough to face another life through reincarnation? Or shall our offended spirits not continue to roam the wild?"

"Enough of these riddles!" exclaimed Professor

Johnson. "They rob us of the desire to live. They leave us hopeless."

"Isn't it better than to perish neglecting the threat of extinction by the white man?" bellowed another elder. "Surely, it is better to die courageously enjoying ourselves than to die several times in anticipation of the so-called civilised world's canons of destruction!"

"Who said they are firing canons?" Obi Nwaka's voice boomed. "Didn't Professor speak of gas masks? Do we have any such invention? Who among you here even has the means to protect himself from as little as a harmless fart?"

"Then to Izu Hall let the youths go . . . As our ancestors would have it, there is enough stock for all!" Pa Okekumatulor enthused.

"Remember, kinsmen, the oldest is not always the wisest," Professor Johnson objected yet again.

"Let it be as the elders have said," Ekwenuya, the scourge of the village intoned. "Fortunately, there is enough for all as Diokpa has rightly noted. Fate couldn't have been kinder. Our ancestors couldn't have been more understanding. All that stuff amassed for our annual purification festival will more than serve for this end of the world party.

NOW! To Izu Hall march all stalwarts who consider themselves men of honour enough," concluded Ekwenuya, bowing before Pa Okekumatulor.

"Action speaks louder than voice," said Pa Okekumatulor as the youths trailed behind Ekwenuya who was now trotting toward Izu Hall. "May our blessings be with you as you arrange our hall."

"So be it," chorused the elders.

"May we never be witnesses to our land's abomination," prayed Pa Okekumatulor.

"So be it," chorused the elders.

"May our ancestors be our chaperons tonight."

"So be it."

"May they remove all drawbacks, for only cowards fear the masquerade dance."

"So be it."

"So be it, O gods of the land!"

"So be it!"

As the youths, led by Ekwenuya, frenziedly arranged Izu Hall, it struck the two philosophy students at the state university that a certain *disease* had actually afflicted the people. Identifying the *disease* as 'gullibility,' Chiedu compared it with that which informed the regrettable Guyana genocide.

"But they can't impose their irrational decision on us." Oni shuddered as he and Chiedu sullenly left the scene, their hands interlocked. "Well, had that so-called Aksion Governor not shut our school, perhaps we would have been spared this unfortunate ordeal of being witnesses to this most absurd . . . what was it called again?"

"END OF THE WORLD PARTY," Chiedu shouted. Then he broke into his favourite refrain again, joined by Oni:

Messiah will come again
After the argument in heaven
Messiah will come again. . .

Their voices were not in the least mellifluous, and nobody seemed to care for their provocative chorus. No one turned back. The earth, draped in shawls of uncertainty, was warming up to a chorus of night birds and the chirruping of night insects. The villagers, inspired by Pa Okekumatulor, and the youths, galvanised by Ekwenuya, were determined to give themselves, as a notable diviner had put it, a "befitting send-off to the great beyond."

Well, had the town crier not said that one burnt star is enough for a child? And, had a self-appointed spokesman not asked his neighbour, "Are seven suicides in forty-eight hours and an imminent apocalypse not too much to handle?"

"Our people have become the riders of the apocalypse which the Holy Book speaks of," Chiedu lamented.

"We shall survive the storm!"

A vicious chill ran through Oni's veins as they entered St. Leo's Catholic Church located in the heart of the village.

"Lord, we have come in search of a miracle," Chiedu prayed.

"Lord, receive our. . ."

"Better die enjoying yourself than peeling off your knees in a church." The distant voice of a faceless creature interrupted Oni before he could add 'prayers.'

Brushing the 'satanic intrusion' aside, he rejoined Chiedu in the prayers.

Meanwhile, the villagers had assembled at Izu Hall. They were surveying each other, surveying the symmetrical arrangement of benches the youths had laid out. They came in their best clothes, carefully chosen from the reserves at the bottom of their boxes. Only the best, the elders had insisted, was suitable for the last masquerade dance, the dance of death, of bidding farewell to a benighted existence.

Group by group, family by family, age group by age group they all sat, discussing in hushed tones. But an hour after the drinks made the rounds, their voices began to rise. A zestful euphoria enveloped the hall. Passions tangled; passions rose. People were carousing, hugging, laughing, dancing, drinking. Long-term enemies pulled together. "Mending our fences," they said. For all, there could not have been a more propitious time for reconciliation and merriment than before the Desert Stormers plunged the world into an abyss.

Still disturbed, Chiedu and Oni left the church only to be confronted with deserted streets and the stubborn echoes of the noises emanating from the End of the World Party at Izu Hall. The moon had gone under the clouds, making way for pitch darkness to reign. There were no shadows, no trees. Only the blurred outline of a few houses without lights could be seen. It was as if nature were still, encapsulating the two 'rebels' in the pith of an iroko tree. But with their conditioned imagination, they traced their way to Oni's place.

As was to be expected, the members of his family had gone to the party. With the eyes of one accustomed to his home, Oni reached the kitchen to fetch a box of matches and search for a lantern. Chiedu remained outside the house, conversing with the darkness and listening to what kept reaching his ears as ghost music from a ghost town.

Suddenly, a flicker of light! Suddenly, from somewhere around the house he heard a strange crow resembling that of the early cock at the break of dawn. As he strained his ears, Oni emerged with the light—just in time to unfreeze him from the spot where he stood, totally overwhelmed by fright.

"Let's not go inside the house," Oni suggested. "Let's sit down here and count down—"

"You believe Saddam and Bush would play out this drama while humanity just awaits its own annihilation?"

"Nothing is impossible."

"With God, you must add," Chiedu said. "Remember the Deluge? Remember Noah's Ark? Oni, don't you believe in the Lord's miracles? We shall be saved, saved, Oni . . . SAVED!"

"AMEN. . ."

"Amen!" a voice in the dark chorused with Oni. "Better die enjoying yourself than peeling off your knees." The sonorous treble, seemingly enriched by the dialect appeared to produce a strange, soporific effect on Chiedu and Oni who began to sing yet again:

Messiah will come again
After the argument in heaven
Messiah will come again. . .

Moments afterwards, Oni shook his head vigorously. He stretched out his hand to pick up the lantern. The lantern seemed to be a kilometre away. Realising he had actually kept it further than he had thought, he rose from the pavement and picked up the lantern. And the creature appeared! Behold, Juliet, the popular half-mad form three drop-out, had unbelievably traced them. Oni adjusted the light to show her up properly. Her innocent smile, enabling her cheeks to depress into a lovely pair of dimples, revealed an immaculate set of teeth that could enchant any man. But her shaggy hair and scaly skin…

As if disturbed by the pin-point sharpness of Juliet's nipples which were emphasised by the nylon texture of her ruffled pink dress, certain thoughts buzzed in Oni's mind like homeless bees.

"Juliet, what do you want here?" Oni coolly asked, gathering the strands of his flying thoughts.

"The party. They chased me away!"

"And so what?" It was Chiedu's turn.

"Let's . . . have . . . our own . . . fun here. I've been so long in the cold." Her voice was sincere, passionate and cool all at once.

"What?" Chiedu was alarmed.

"Well, better die enjoying yourself than peeling off your knees—" The now familiar expression sunk into the two friends with new fangs. The words were raw, as raw as the flesh of a prey being devoured by a lion. The words shot through Chiedu's heart, leaving him bleeding with incoherent words:

"Desert storm . . . passion . . . party . . . enjoyment . . . peeling . . . coitus . . ."

"Open the door and let me in; even a stray dog finds food," Juliet pleaded as the wind drove her loose pink gown up her thighs. Against the wind, its pleats whispered in protest.

"Oni, let us survive together," she bellowed.

A silent assessment of her disturbing presence and words abandoned Oni, also robbing Chiedu of the gift of speech.

Juliet stood before them, her beautiful face assuming the outline of *Tutu's* as rendered by the deft, artful hands of the master artist, Ben Enwonwu.

"What could be wrong? Isn't this girl mad anymore? Doesn't she know what she's doing? Isn't she saner than all those at Izu Hall—?" The torrent of questions soaked Chiedu and Oni, and their faces were soddened with sympathy. They sat, stone still, admiring Juliet's alluring and experienced innocence.

And time ticked away as fear of the expected demise of the world at dawn stole on Oni, intuitively preventing him from looking at his timepiece.

Not unexpectedly, the same feeling prevailed on the villagers at the party. Nobody bothered about TIME since everything appeared to have been decided. Oblivious of what was still happening in the neighbourhood, Juliet was enjoying her sleep by the pavement, on one side of which Oni and Chiedu were keeping vigil.

As the first streaks of another dawn filtered from the sky, the town crier's gong distracted the villagers. He was delivering Professor Johnson's message. The town crier had stolen away from the End of the World Party in search of knowledge at the wizened academic's residence.

The rush to Professor Johnson's following the town crier's announcement betrayed the villagers' rekindled anxiety. . .

"Can we talk sense now?" Professor Johnson asked the crowd as he turned down the volume of his radio.

"Say, Prof, what has V.O.A. said again?" Ekwenuya hurriedly violated the ensuing silence.

"Look," Professor Johnson began as a little sleepyhead slumped to the ground, "America and her allies have attacked Iraq . . . and as you can see, the effect of the war has not, will not reach these parts. . ."

The words, momentarily trapped in midair, sounded hollow to the villagers. Then, Pa Okekumatulor and his Council of Elders knew that they might never find enough courage to look the Professor in the face again. REALITY seized all, purging them of whatever illusions had filled their minds. With the rays of daylight emerging from the brightening sky like fresh buds, the villagers seemed to be waking from a drugged past. They began to realise how absurd their acts had been, how it had been hanging in a balance like a fool's affair.

As they returned to their houses, sober like the

proverbial prodigal son, Chiedu and Oni's refrain continued to renew their consciousness with divine hope:

Messiah will come again
After the argument in heaven
Messiah will come again. . .

THE *lyric laced Onwuka's mind with a new understanding. As he walked back to his writing desk that Saturday morning, he realised how far reality had been distorted in his imagination, among others, conflating Operation Desert Shield and Operation Desert Storm. He pondered how the story had come to occupy his mind as he stared at the world through the window of his room in Premier University. "Well, without stories the world will collapse," he intoned a local proverb as he began to trap the story in his memo book. And he did so as fast as he could so that he could go and join his friends at the Students' Union building where, besides talking about women and books as usual, they would talk world politics*

and the end of the 'Father of all Defeats' that day in 1991, months after an apocalypse was predicted.

One Day In The Life Of An Applicant

Every step reminds
You of the spiralling queues
Of jobless youths rotting
In the rain like orange rinds.

— *Esiaba Irobi*

I was travelling in a *danfo* overloaded with people. Beside me in the front seat was a young nursing mother. She delicately held her son in her arms. The reckless mini-bus driver carelessly drove into a pothole, one of the numerous potholes along that road. The baby was nearly thrown from his mother's arms.

"*Ha! Ha! Ha! Ha!*" cackled a man. He wore a navy-blue overall which he seemed to cherish like a memorial tribute. "Bomboy, dat na potholes wey you go fall put tire for life," he burst into an unsolicited commentary directed at the infant. "You no see? Everywhere, every road, na so-so bump-bump. This road na road of life. These potholes na the wahala wey full am. So, bomboy, no vex o." As he uttered these words, he tightened the skin on his face sullenly like a man going to a funeral.

A sibilant sound escaped from the nursing mother's mouth. She wanted to say something, but she censored the words that were battling to escape from her bloated lips.

"Madam, you no fit talk?" a quarrelsome woman, perhaps in her early thirties, asked. "Na so dem dey put bad mout' for wetin wey no concern dem."

"My sister, na true the man talk bo. Wetin you dey quarrel with am for?" retorted the nursing mother.

"It's all right!" I intervened, then looked back, peering into the mournful faces in the bus. "You know what? A musician has tried to capture our nation's problem. He said they are potholes, bumps, uniforms and gates. He said that if we're not running into bumps or falling into potholes, we'll be running into uniformed men of the force, or into gates that are closed to us. And that is true! See how one of these potholes nearly snuffed the life out of this boy. Very soon one of those men of authority in uniform will be harassing us for one reason or the other. Even the private security men in uniform have the power entrenched in the *almighty* uniforms to harass the poor. The other day, a member of the Boy Scouts molested me for cautioning a colleague of his in *mufti* for violating a *W.A.I.** code. That's our life—ruled by uniforms, bumps, potholes, or menacing gates and 'signboasts'. What a pity!"

"That na true," supported one of the passengers. "Signposts no dey Nigeria again. Na 'signboasts' full everywhere. Even my Cameroonian girlfriend commented on it."

"You see, like that musician rightly pointed out," I continued, "every Big Man's place in this country is encased in high walls like the Great Wall of China. Somewhere on the fence an iron curtain proclaims: BEWARE OF DOGS or SECURITY DOGS ON PATROL or DANGER, ELECTRIFIED FENCE. One eccentric man was even said to have posted BEWARE OF SNAKES on his."

"Dem dey give those big-big dogs plenty food, come still pay watchday and watchnight," the artisan said. "Na tief dem all dey tief the money o."

"It's not all of them that steal," quipped I.

"Dem go fit make those kain money without cheating?" persisted the artisan.

"That's all right," I said.

There were murmurings!

"Allow me to continue," I pleaded.

Silence prevailed. Most of the passengers looked eager to hear more of my social sermon.

"Ehen . . . if it is not that kind of physical gate, it is the gate their receptionists mount. To the 'wretched of the earth', it's always . . . ehm . . . M.D. is not on seat!"

Excited by my clever simulation of those uncouth receptionists' voice, the passengers burst into mirthful laughter which tore through my dream, resounding in my head like an endless echo.

I looked round the congested, cheerless room. By the help of the faint rays of light from the open window, I saw Onochie and Jeko still snoring by my side on the floor. On the dilapidated bed, Sunny and Debo lay, talking in whispers.

"Good day," I greeted them in my usual way. Both of them, like the rest of us, were unemployed graduates.

"May your wish come true," retorted Sunny who was the oldest of us all living in that dingy room.

The room had been rented by Debo's elder brother who had died of cardiac arrest. We had joined Debo as very close friends in crushing need of a place to lay our heads while we looked for jobs. We had come to Lagos from our villages in search of better opportunities.

"How often do we experience a good day?" Onochie asked, scratching his scrotum absentmindedly. I neglected his touching question and rose from the dirty mattress on the floor. I made for the switch beside the door then remembered that the power had been cut off by *NEPA*.* So, to get my soap container, I relied on the rays of light peeping into our room from the security light in Mr. Ojupu's compound.

I hurried into the dirty bathroom and scrubbed my body clean of the stale sweat which had merged with dust particles that had stuck to my body during the previous day's street beating. Then I returned to the room and put on the pair of trousers I had worn the previous day. I looked round, found one good-looking shirt, slipped my lean trunk into it and finished up my dressing by running a near-toothless comb through my damp hair.

As the room was being overtaken by the wide

effulgence of a rising sun, I hastened out into the world.

There were lots of young men and women already skulking in the crowded bus stop. I firmly gripped the copy of Festus Iyayi's novel, *Violence,* which I had taken along with me. It contained my world's treasure: my credentials which I had tucked into a small, brown envelope.

A *molue* pulled up. As it slowed down it groaned noisily, shattering—along with the calls of conductors and the noises made by passengers as they clambered strenuously into the moving bus—the eerie quietness of the early morning. I contested entrance into the bus with others. I succeeded. But I had to stand. The bus was already crammed with people, some spilling out the doors and hanging precariously with one hand.

The odour inside the bus was nauseating. It stung my nose. It made me dizzy for a moment or so. As the dizziness dissipated, I felt trickles of sweat on my forehead. Yet it was still early in the morning when the coolness of the weather normally soothes human bodies like sea breeze.

"*Owo e da?*" the conductor, a stocky, late teenager with scars on his face, asked in Yoruba for my fare. I dipped my right hand into my pocket while my left hand where I had the novel still clung to the pole above my head. I clinched two naira and gave it to the conductor.

The *molue* kept moving, punctuating the journey at bus stops to drop off or pick up yet more hardy passengers.

Not quite long afterwards, we arrived at the Marina area of the city, which one may say is the unofficial commercial nerve centre of Lagos. We all jumped out of the bus one after the other as it groaned to a jerky stop. I looked around, then strolled to a rather remote corner. I opened the novel in my hand and found the business card. I glanced at the address and nodded. Then I peered at a passer-by's wristwatch. It was twenty-six minutes past nine. I was almost late for the 9.30 appointment. And how was I to explain that I had left home quite early, but had been delayed by the constant stops of the bus and the notorious Eko Bridge *go slow**?

"Please, do you know where Nation Builder's Consult office is?" I asked a man who was hawking *okirika*.

"Take this road . . . pass the first junction, the second one. If you reach that third one wey green and white signboard dey, turn left. Before you waka like . . . ehm . . . two poles, you go see'am."

"Thank you."

I hurried along the direction. On the third turning to the left, I saw the wide signboard of the company about eighteen metres away:

NATION BUILDERS CONSULT LIMITED
BEST BUILDING TECHNOLOGISTS & CIVIL ENGINEERS
1135A, MARTIN STREET, LAGOS.
WE BLAZE THE TRAIL, OTHERS FOLLOW.

If the words amused or enthused me, I would not know. But I smiled to myself for some obscure reasons. The throbbing of my heart increased as I got to the entrance of BUILDERS HOUSE. The massive door was like some artist's impression of heaven's gate. I obeyed the instruction posted on the door: I pulled and went into the hall.

At a strategic corner, on the inside left corner of the hall, was lodged the receptionist's desk, a solid mass of mahogany. Behind it was a petite, old-cargo-type lady also known in popular parlance as a Senior Girl. Although she appeared to have been scoured by weathering and by men, she still showed traces of a once striking beauty.

"Good morning," I greeted in a measured tone, trying, as it were, to sound only as audible as was necessary.

"Morning," she acknowledged hesitantly. "Yes, can I help you?"

I placed the complimentary card on the table. "The Managing Director asked me to see him today at this time."

"Where did you meet the M.D.? Anyway, the M.D. is not on seat. Try another time," she said with a tone of finality and a humiliating, vacant gaze.

I was stupefied, for I had mistaken the matronly look in her eyes for understanding. Now I stood sweating profusely before her. I was still; my feet glued to the floor, my mouth agape.

Just then, a robust man with conspicuous folds of skin on his neck slouched up to the desk. I realised that my mouth was still open so I shut it, absorbing the man's appearance. Apart from the thick folds of skin on the visitor's short neck, his protuberant belly overlapped his belt. He was, you may say, as round as a football.

"Good morning, sir," greeted the receptionist, standing up at the same time. As I was quickly pondering how such a seemingly wealthy man could not afford to take care of his appearance, the man spoke.

"Hello, fine girl." There was an alluring look in his dull eyes.

The rotten odour which issued from the man's mouth impinged on my breath for a moment. It stank like fart emitted by a man who had eaten a lot of beans and eggs. I spontaneously stepped aside. The receptionist did not seem to perceive the stinking odour that wafted out of the man's mouth. Or perhaps she did but pretended that it may all have been part of the money bag's designer perfume.

"You want to see Oga?" she asked with a remarkable eagerness to help the man with the smelling mouth.

"That's right! I want to see CHIEF!" he said.

"Okay, just a minute."

She had hardly finished talking than she began to dial a number.

"Sir, an important visitor for you . . . Chief . . . ehm . . ." The man tossed his dust-coloured business card on the well-polished table, which it seemed to stain.

"Ehm . . . Chief Okobio, the General Manager of Ekwensu Enterprises Limited."

The man with the rotten mouth was ushered by the receptionist into a poshly furnished room which I glimpsed as he struggled through the doorway.

No longer able to bear her mistreatment, I decided to vent my anger.

"You're a blatant, shameless liar," I said with all the boldness I could muster as she picked up the receiver of the ringing phone. "To hell with your *inyanga** and your Nation whatever. To hell with your kind, and the kinds of that man with rotten mouth which you couldn't even smell because you were too busy fawning to him. Is that how you build the nation here? Through injustice. . .?"

"That's your business. Is it my fault that you aren't a VIP? If you. . ."

"Very Important Pig indeed!" I hissed and walked out on her. I walked along the street, much aggrieved by the fact that that semi-literate receptionist and that round man did things the way they liked right inside that 'Destroyers House.' It struck me that that was yet another obituary opportunity. But I hardly cared then. What hurt me most was that that opportunity would inevitably be clinched by one of the children of the likes of that man with the rotten mouth. I started then to grow very bitter;

for there is nothing quite so frustrating as rattling along the noisy and riotous streets of Lagos looking endlessly for employment and encountering those rotten Vagabonds In Power.

I kept on walking, drenched in sweat. The sun had begun to shoot its piercing darts on the earth. It was gradually becoming hot like a furnace. Yet, it was that time of the year in tropical countries when the earth was usually cooled by the harmattan.

I stopped walking. Instinctively, I glanced at my body. My faded clothes clung stubbornly to my lean frame. Anger kept looming in my chest like some dense cloud about to burst into a heavy down-pour. Around me, people kept milling like working ants—but less organised than working ants. Most of them impressed me as hustlers.

I made a detour. Walked a few metres more and stopped to read a signpost. It was quite an absorbing one. It persuaded me to try my luck for any vacant post in the building.

It was a magnificent building sandwiched between two other skyscrapers along Broad Street. As I walked into the building, I met one of my schoolmates. He looked rather unhealthy. His once fleshy body had withered away. His lanky frame with its screaming bones seemed to be announcing that he was SUFFERING. His head, like some ants', was conspicuously bigger than the rest of his body. One would have mistaken him for a refugee! But I knew . . . And how was I sure I had not become equally emaciated. I could not but follow him out of the building into the street. I had not seen him since we left school two and a half years ago. Besides, he might have valuable newspaper cuttings of adverts for vacancies which I hadn't seen, I thought.

"Ol' boy, the weather's been too hostile to son of man." He spoke as if there was a lump in his throat.

"Jigs Bobs, you're not alone in the hostile times. Can't you see that the roses are withering while the weeds are blooming?"

"Ol' boy, you've not forgotten your poetry? Man, I've been living in Hell. And there's no poetry in Hell, if you know what I mean."

The tooting horn of a snack vendor diverted his attention. The man was meandering professionally through the maze of pedestrians and cars along the street. He looked at the showcase hungrily. I did too! Then I began to salivate like a starving downtown *Isale Eko* area boy who had smelt food. I suppose I heard Jigide's stomach rumble for the edibles it had learnt were nearby. As if in answer to a bard's call, mine responded with a huff. We looked at each other with understanding.

"Snacks!" I beckoned to the man.

"Yes, hot snacks—meat pie, eggroll . . . and cold *minerals** here."

"How much?" Jigide asked, pointing accusingly at a pie.

"One-one naira."

"Okay," I said, "Jigs, I have only five naira on me. I'll need the two *card* to at least get me near home, then I trek the remaining two or so kilometres from the bus stop. Add one naira so we can buy two bottles of Coke to wash down the pies. But, by the way, Oga snacks, are these meat pies or potato pies or yam pies?"

The man hissed and smiled almost at the same time.

"I have just fifty kobo more than my transport fare. I am—"

"Jigs, that's all right. We'll buy two pies and a bottle of water to wash it down then." I paid for the pies.

Jigide tossed the fifty kobo coin into the bucket of bottles of cold water being sold by a little girl.

She gave him a Lucozade bottle filled with water.

"Man, this is my brunch," Jigide said as we munched away like gorillas. He still had not forgotten how we qualified a meal of breakfast and lunch rolled into one at school. We finished our 'fast meal' and reverted to our old discussion.

"Ol' boy, it's terribly tough . . . It's hectic," Jigide said, stroking his wiry beard. "You know what? My dad was retrenched about four months ago and he has seven other children to train. Of course, you know my mum is dead. Man! It's death we are facing." He moaned. He swallowed the lump in his throat.

"Easy does it, Jigs! It's the same everywhere. You remember the highlife tune: *Where there is life, there is hope*"?

"Ol' boy, it's not the same. It's easy for the oppressors: THEM," said Jigide.

"Imagine! That Shaibu Mallam has secured a job—a good job—with the *NNPC**! But here we are, combing the streets of Lagos for employment, even employment as clerks!"

"Jigs my brother, it's a tale of one nation, WORN naira, different destinies; and the citizenry pursuing unity in their destinies."

"What elusive unity can there be? With nepotism wreaking disunity? With mediocrity being installed through the so-called quota system to overtake meritocracy while we stand aside and look? With the military and their civilian collaborators subjecting us to an endless and wasteful transition to their so-called home-grown democratic rule programme? What unity? With all the religious persecution? Why unity? With a culture of monopoly of power? Why not. . ." Jigide got instantly immersed in a diatribe against the system. He was absorbed like an evangelist, nodding self-approval intermittently.

We must have stood there for a considerable period, chatting away about our grievances against the establishment, for my legs soon began to ache. But I had managed to stay on, sharing our woeful existence, undisturbed by the tooting of vehicles' horns, the screeching tyres of automobiles and the blah-blah of passers-by, all of which reached a sickening decibel that pointed to a destructive, chaotic existence which Lagosians had grown addicted to, and had learnt to enjoy!

I brushed the sweat off my face with one edge of the novel in my hand while still sustaining my intense gaze on Jigide. I could hear the tempest of rage in his heart even in that noisy environment. His dour emotions infected me, or so it seemed: an ineffable anger entrenched itself solidly in a portion of my disjointed mind. My mind was boiling like a *mama-put's** soup. Oh, it had become a hot spring of sadness! The more I looked at Jigide, the angrier I became. My anger grew in leaps like molten magma about to erupt. Jigide stood still. I stood still. And time ticked away unconcernedly. And people kept hustling for their living while we kept talking about the living that was slipping away from us.

"Jigs, these problems may never be solved," I said sadly. "Not by our anger!" I added in a sudden flash of realisation. "For how long have we been angry? And for how long shall we continue to criticise the system without acting?"

"Ol' boy, I am tired. Stiff tired! Must we remain hostages to unemployment and hunger and all forms of malaise?"

"Why must our people not be violent?" I had hardly finished asking the rhetorical question than a big Volvo car breezed dangerously past us, almost snatching us from the improvised pavement.

"Thanks be to God," uttered Jigide rather unconsciously while making the sign of the Cross. "I think we'd better go home."

"Before we end up being employed by our ancestors," I quipped, and we laughed. "Hope to see you some other time." Jigide extended his right hand for a parting handshake.

It was not particularly my pleasure shaking hands. It had lost all its meaning and had been reduced to a tiresome ritual. But I took Jigide's hand reluctantly and squeezed his fingers gently and urgently.

"It's been a pleasure sharing with you," he purred.

"Oh! I'm glad. It's different from the disappointments one encounters in those offices. Jigs, it's been like an embrocation, very soothing after the annoying massage."

As Jigide disappeared into the crowd, I trotted after a *molue* whose conductors were calling out my route.

At that time, the crowd had tripled; more people were still pouring out of offices and besieging the streets. The now crimson sun had travelled to a low angle in the sky. The still air was dominated by the acrid odour of fumes puffing out of the engines of old, misused vehicles and the clashing smell of perfumes, deodorants, body odours, *et cetera*. As I trotted after the *molue* with the strength of a man who had eaten only a piece of 'dough' with half a bottle of water, I heard Fela Anikulapo Kuti's *Original Sufferhead* blaring from a Volkswagen Beetle. The driver, a seemingly tall, square-shouldered, middle-aged man was swaying his small head rhythmically to the tune.

At last, I caught the bus and anchored myself precariously on the jamb of the rear door then wriggled my way to stand properly just inside the *molue*, not far from the ever-open door. The *molue* hollered on.

Soon, I began to jerk my head sleepily. It was as if my energies had been spent in the same way the steam in an electric steam iron is spent. But somehow, the nose-splitting odour that an excrement-ridden, brackish pond we were driving by around the National Theatre emitted, combining with the odour from the bus, kept me awake. I managed to peep outside: daylight was gradually embracing dusk. Somewhere along the skyline, the low clouds looked like wisps of smoke rotating joyfully in concentric rings. Beside the bush, by the roadside, a man was defecating nonchalantly. And nobody cared, or so it seemed. It reminded me of what I had heard one environmental expert say: "In Lagos, every roadside bush is a putative toilet."

I chuckled.

When the *molue* got to the bus stop where I had to get down, I wormed my way through the human obstruction at the door and jumped down. Among others, an old woman skilfully climbed down from the bus, staggered a little, then gained balance.

"Condukitor *shange mi da?*" she asked, extending a trembling hand to collect her balance from the crooked conductor.

I glanced askance at the conductor and began to walk in the direction of the hovel where I was squatting.

"Oh God! Can't you see?" I muttered as I plodded along, remembering Ezeanah's moving lines:

And you say God sees these things?
And you say I should not cry?

After walking a few metres, I got home. I knocked. There was no reply. I raised the dusty footmat and took the key. I slipped it into its hole and opened the door. The room was hot as usual. I pulled off my worn-out shoes, stripped off totally, then slumped onto the aged bed. It shrieked in protest, but what did it matter?

I shut my dull eyes to mull over the day. I was struck by a sudden realisation: the day had, like other dragon-ridden days one was getting used to, risen, and it was now setting like wild hopes.

But life continues. . .

And some alien voices in my tired head kept on droning: "This ritual will end someday. . ."

Afterword

Nduka Otiono and the Frontiers of African Narrativity

Frank Uche Mowah[1]

FOR too long, interest in fostering a distinct school of Nigerian fiction with its roots sunk and buried in the lore of our historical experience has been a mere anthropological fascination. Students of African fiction and story-telling art content themselves with itemizing the features of orality present in certain works and leaving the rest for folklorists to garner as antiquarian evidence.

In the search for a unique Nigerian narrative technique, for indeed it is in the narrative genre that distinction can ever be made between one people's literature and another, we must burrow deep into the creative resource and possibilities of our society's master narrators.

---

1. Dr. Frank Uche Mowah was a writer and Head of Department of English, Edo State University (now Ambrose Alli University), Ekpoma. He died on November 13, 1998. This essay, adopted for the Afterword of the twenty-fifth anniversary edition of *The Night Hides with a Knife*, was first presented at the formal launch of the book on July 9, 1996. The event was held at the main auditorium of the Nigeria Institute of International Affairs in Lagos.

Nduka Otiono in *The Night Hides with a Knife* which won the first ANA/Spectrum prize for fiction does exactly just that. The ten carefully crafted stories in the collection exemplify a successful synthesis of the oral and the written forms in Nigerian literary tradition to produce a useful new strategy for coping with the post-modernist demands in an age of information technology.

Nweke Momah's accomplished technique serves Otiono well as a perfect model. Otiono craftily reconstructs Momah's prototypes by forging ahead to produce blueprints of the contemporary interdependence between the phonocentric (the voices without and within the machine) and the written or printed to extend the frontiers of narrativity in Nigerian fiction. Narrativity in this sense implying how the text can read itself and allow the participating readers to follow it.

Perhaps there is a need to mention a few things about Nweke Momah for the sake of those who do not know him. He was a remarkable artist, storyteller and composer who began life as a valet in the court of the Obi of Ubulu Uku in Aniocha area of Delta State. He rose to prominence, fame and recognition in the Igbo speaking area of the then Bendel State through his performing group made up of female chorus dancers. His narrative technique is simple but complex. He provides the theme of the story with an opening matrix which may be a proverb, an epigram, a quotation or a simple couplet. The chorus responds with their simple musical instruments, maracas, drum and flutes and song. The story then unfolds through the song and dance movements until it reaches a climactic point where the female dancers dominate the central circle and become the focal point of the audience. Even though Momah is celebrated as a famous storyteller, what most of his critics and researchers tend to overlook is the fact that his art is a source of empowerment to women as well as to the marginalized of his society, and by implication, to all those worsted in the power tussle of existence.

Momah's interest in women is that of a composer who is fascinated by the ambiguous images of the siren she represents to members of his society. We must therefore distinguish between the ontological resource artist (composer) in the oral setting and the narrator or performer If we are to appreciate the pains Otiono has taken in his stories, especially in stories such as "Just Before the Desert Storm" and

"The Night Hides with a Knife" which remind us of the place of imagination in the composition of artistic works as against the often taken- for-granted notion of spontaneity, improvisation and performance which are foregrounded in stories like "Wings of Rebellion" and "Jubilant Flames," stories which demonstrate the new place of orality in the postmodern age of information technology.

Momah's focus on women is a conscious study of the art and method of the archetypal composer who for an inexplicable twist of perception is denigrated by the society as an object of insignificance, yet this denigrated image stands eternally as the symbol of what is sacrosanct in the society. It is not for fun that in the search for a lucid symbol of black aesthetics, the conjure woman was reincarnated in Black literature. She had to be brought back from the grave of the memory of the African experience.

This is because she was the one who worked in the farm, cooked in the homestead after the day's labour, and sold in the market woven cloths, tended the sick through her art of healing, midwifed the birth of endless tales which she wove from her daily experiences of being the balm for soothing wounded and aching minds of members of her society.

And in the struggle for survival and emancipation in the slave-ridden America, it was this woman's spirit that soared indomitably.

In Aniocha-Oshimili area of Delta State of Nigeria, as indeed in every Nigerian society, this woman is faceless and is still taken for granted except if you contemplated her long enough as Otiono had to do when he started gathering materials for his MA dissertation. I became aware of this when we started discussing some of his findings during some of those story-telling sessions as S.U.B. bar which he vividly re-enacts in the story entitled "Wings of Rebellion." The pattern which was wittingly or unwittingly forming in his mind then was ravishingly stimulating to me because unknown to him he had opened my eyes to my own reality. The picture which he was painting, and which had been illusive was that of my own mother.

And the picture is that the woman who composes and spins tales is invariably a weaver or a cloth maker. But she is also many things in one. A market woman, sometimes a teacher or a nurse, a farmer, and a mother. She weaves intricate patterns of images on her cloth, abstracts of the unfolding experience in her world. But as it were, she is consciously trying to plot these images into a meaning as she repeats the pattern again and again until it becomes impressed on the mind of the society that adorns the cloth. Then, on a certain evening under the illumination of the moonlight, WAMBAM! The story explodes. It shoots out of her mind as a memorable fable or as an allegory, or as a traditional narrative. Stories about political naivete in the society, or about inept and corrupt leaders, or about a hungry youth who broke into a yam barn and was caught, about young girls seduced by the glittering city lights, about ill-gotten wealth, about witchcraft and others. Without realizing it, this preparer of evening meals for her family had become a myth-maker as well as the unacclaimed legislator of the society.

This is why Nweke Momah formed a dominantly female dance group. He introduces a matrix of narration and the women dance singing, spinning endless, tales about the society's valuable experiences.

Similarly, in Otiono's work, he presents in every story, a matrix taken from a poet or a visioner and the "women" begin to dance, doing intricate motifs of the experiences of living in modern Nigeria, alerting us of the hidden daggers in the darkness of our souls.

The title story, "The Night Hides with a Knife" appears to be the least accomplished in terms of plot and resolution of conflict. But this is deliberate. First because it immediately warns us about the journalistic immediacy of the short story in a society that is ridden by crises. But more importantly, because it stands at the gate of the entire collection as a guide to the structure of discourse, reminding us from the onset that a story is indeed a hidden knife that cuts in the dark chambers of our minds both ways, revealing the multiple fractures of our experiences, personalities, and society. This is a never-ending ritual which subverts the closing lines of the collection that 'This ritual will end someday."

All the stories in the collection begin with a tragic cry, evoking the abyss of darkness in its various synecdochic possibilities. Thunder, lightning, darkness, dark cloud, night, drunkenness, etc. These lure the reader into a realistic realm of surprise, failure, defeat and hopelessness.

Death is omnipresent but is rendered insignificant by the more tragic assaults of natural political forces which turn the characters into victims, and turn the atmosphere into a gruesome, hostile, un-endurable hell.

The stories cover a wide range of our contemporary experiences. They appear familiar because they re-enact for us the living drama of our sordid lives in modern day Nigeria, but certainly the stories are not worn or banal, instead they are renewed with fresh images, with clearer vision, and profound insight into our national dilemma. The most tragic and acrid story is the first one in the collection entitled "A Will to Survive." In this story, man is transformed into a pathetic delirious degenerate. A living corpse, a worm unable to go beyond the last stage of its metamorphoses. What the man considers to be a survival instinct is a mere insignificant gesture that even attracts the sympathy of the victim of robbery. This story is complemented by the last story in the collection "One Day in the Life of an Applicant" which vividly transforms the mordant diary of an applicant into a biting metaphor of the hopelessness, and the stunted future of our country's university graduates. In this country, only the corrupt and evil survive like the character in "Fatal Birth" who thrives on the blood of his unborn child. Honest and hardworking young persons like Suleiman, the cobbler, in the very fine story, "Jubilant Flames," are stretched by the society's savagery to the fatal limit of endurance.

"Wings of Rebellion" means exactly what it says. A flight into the realm of artistic possibilities. In this story, Otiono brings in everything in his artistic repertoire to bear, he presents us an exquisite finish of an example of the phonocentric tradition of literature in the African context, of how voices are entrapped in the artificial memory of the tape recorder as every image spins in a spiral of recollection, involvement, digressions, distractions and reflection. "Wings of Rebellion" subverts the postmodern assertion of meaninglessness and that postmodernity has not, in fact, rendered the text an empty technology.

"Wings of Rebellion" is about licentiousness, about the reckless immorality in our society. The story is about what the shapely thighs do to the mind of the average Nigerian male; it is about profligacy, the bane of our existence and the cause of our national dilemma, the reason behind why men neglect both their filial and social responsibilities. It is the old story of harlotry retold through the eyes of the participating members of the audience, but in this instance, Otiono rightly puts the blame on the man who exploits the woman for his own gratification. It is thus, a revisit of the womanist vision which informed the vision of Nweke Momah. It is aptly described as "A Fool's Affair" because no male who can achieve an erection is left out. The storyteller does leave us in no doubt about that when he admonishes members of his audience some of whom are already drooling with lust: "Keep laughing! you might as well be laughing at our man." This admonition extends to all the other stories and presents us with the very important goal of Otiono's stories: To see ourselves the way we are in the mirror, to give us advice in a "form that becomes inseparable from (our) whole self."

All the stories in *The Night Hides with a Knife* deal in a metaphorical manner with the theme of our socio-political problems. The stories are a reflection of the author's aesthetic commitment to our socio-economic malaise. They betray Otiono's anger at the misrule in our country which has bred unemployment, incarceration of the innocent, prostitution, dereliction of duty, hunger, exploitation, suicide, and corruption.

Otiono's language is poetically beautiful and

captivating. It is fluid with piquant, sensuous and sensual images that lead us straight into the hidden corners of the human mind. Thus, all the characters whether bots or dynamic, whether protagonist or antagonist become one character, become victims as Otiono progressively tries to work out the ritual of our daily existence in a developing economy. Not ironically, we are left with sizzling smell of emptiness at the end of the ritual exercise.

Nevertheless, the most important issue now is that with this collection, Otiono has affirmed the emergence of a distinct school of Nigerian literature. We are being reminded that the foundation of that school is in the folklore in the culture of the people, that the Nigerian tradition of storytelling has grown from a complex cultural and political matrix out of which Chinua Achebe's and Amos Tutuola's fiction was born and out of which Nigerian fiction will continue to grow. Otiono has also reminded us of the impossibility of creating a new form without the intrusion of the political and socio-economic conditions that are the significant and often tragic aspects of our experience.

The issue in Nigerian fiction is no longer that of good and evil. Our experience in the postmodern and postcolonial times has driven us beyond those fringes. As *The Night Hides With a Knife* has clearly symbolized the issue is that of the beautiful and the ugly, the dark and light, a distinction which must remain foregrounded in the consciousness of every Nigerian in order to remind us of our vanishing beauty and dream as a people.

Glossary

* More definitions of terms used in this book can be found on-line at *Naijalingo: The Nigerian Pidgin English Dictionary.*

Abiku – Yoruba word for a mystery child who keeps reincarnating.

Agbisi – Delta Igbo: A tiny black ant notorious for stinging children who sit with their bare buttocks on the floor in the villages.

Area boy – Notorious layabout commonly roaming parts of Lagos.

Ashawo bastard – An insult that literally suggests a person was born by a prostitute; idiomatically, suggests a scallywag.

Card – Slang word for the Naira, Nigerian currency.

Chuchalacha – Ideophone: At all!

Chicken peri-peri – A kind of malaprop used sometimes to refer to a local delicacy, chicken pepper-soup.

Chineke! – Igbo: God!

Couprintendent – Name ridiculing all uniform-wearing members of the Armed Forces, implying their potential as coup plotters.

Dibia – Igbo: Traditional (herbal) medicine-practitioners, a.k.a. native doctors.

Ganja – Cannabis.

Green khaki boys – Disdainful reference to soldiers.

Go slow – Traffic congestion.

Iddos – Delta-Igbo: Orange-coloured ants found on orange trees, etc.

Igbo – Cannabis. This should not be confused with the Igbo people, East of Nigeria.

Ikebe – Derived from "Ikebe" meaning buttocks, a term largely popularised by a Nigerian comic, Ikebe Super.

Inyanga – Hausa: Pride.

Iwu meal – Sacred meal associated with the Iwu festival and the local stream called Obida in Ogwashi-Uku, the author's hometown.

Jara – Slang for a bonus after a purchase.

Langa-langa – Hausa: A long cutlass typically used for cutting grass.

Kabu-kabu – Unpainted private-car-turned-taxi popular in Nigerian cities as a spin-off of the harsh effects of the Structural Adjustment Programme.

Kpanla – Dried Cod, a delicacy in parts of Nigeria.

Mama-dash-me – A loose-fitting dress handed down to a young girl by her mother.

Mama-put – Local food seller or vendor.

Manya – Igbo: Drink; in this context, alcoholic drink.

Mbanu – Igbo: No, of course not.

Minerals – Popular name for carbonated sodas such as Coke, Pepsi, etcetera.

Mkpakala – Trap for ensnaring mice.

Molue – Often rickety, over-loaded, yellow bus common in Lagos and notorious for its "49 sitting, 99 standing" arrangement satirised by Afrobeat King, Fela Anikulapo Kuti in his song, "Shuffering and Smiling."

Muri-Muri – N20 notes which bear the portrait of late Nigerian ex-military Head of State, General Muritala Muhammed.

NNPC. – Nigeria National Petroleum Corporation.

NEPA – National Electric Power Authority.

Njakili – Igbo: Insulting exchanges.

Nzu – Igbo: Native chalk, either in powdery form as is being referred to here or moulded into balls.

Obida, Ngene, Atachi – Names of streams in Og-washi-Uku, Delta State, Nigeria, believed to be imbued with mystical powers.

Oga – Pidgin: Boss, superior.

Ogbanje – Igbo word for a mystery child who keeps reincarnating.

Okirika – Imported, used items such as clothes, etc.

Okpata – Nonsense. To yarn okpata is to speak recklessly or negatively; to nonsense talk.

Olorun o ma-she! – Yoruba: Lord, what a pity!

Opolo eyes – Ideophone: Big eyes; derived from the Yoruba word for toad, "opolo."

Ota pia pia – A local poisonous concoction that kills and dries mice.

Oyibo – Slang for white people or Caucasians.

Settle: Connotes corrupt practice by which people are compromised. It crept into common usage during the regime of a Nigerian military president infamous for turning it into statecraft.

Shikena – Hausa: That's the end.

Siddon-look – Pidgin: Sit and watch or observe; passivity.

Talakawas – Hausa: Commoners.

U.C.H. – University College Hospital, Ibadan.

W.A.I. – War Against Indiscipline: A programme introduced in Nigeria to sanitise the country by the General Buhari–Idiagbon military regime between 1983 and 1985.

Waka-about shoes – Knockabout shoes.

Wallahi! – Hausa: (exclamation and swear word) I swear!

Wazobia – Amalgam of local words for "come" in Yoruba, Hausa and Igbo which locals use to refer to the N50 note; so-called because it bears portraits representing the three major ethnic groups in Nigeria. Also, used to describe a person who is fluent in the three major languages, that is, Yoruba, Hausa and Igbo.

Wem – Ideophone: Suggesting smooth movement.

Yakata – Ideophone: Suggesting falling apart, carelessly.

419 – Section 419 of the Criminal Code on advance-fee fraud; stealing by false pretence.